In Love with
the King of Harlem

In Love with
the King of Harlem

Jahquel J.

www.urbanbooks.net

Urban Books, LLC
300 Farmingdale Road, NY-Route 109
Farmingdale, NY 11735

In Love with the King of Harlem

ISBN 13: 978-1-62286-134-7
ISBN 10: 1-62286-134-5

First Trade Paperback Printing November 2019
Printed in the United States of America

10 9 8 7 6 5 4 3 2 1

Distributed by Kensington Publishing Corp.
Submit Orders to:
Customer Service
400 Hahn Road
Westminster, MD 21157-4627
Phone: 1-800-733-3000
Fax: 1-800-659-2436

Prologue

Qua

The time stopped and stayed still as I stared in my beautiful wife's eyes. They were red from her crying her eyes out all night and day. Her parents didn't approve of us getting married, but fuck what they thought. This woman was my world, and I loved her with everything in me. Wynner had been by my side through everything and would always be by my side. When you know the shit is real, you make moves to make sure you secure the one who's always going to ride for you. Wynner was that woman for me, and I made sure to call her more than my girl. Now, she was my wife.

"Baby, you my wife now, and you know I got you." My finger wiped the tears out of her eyes. "It's us until the end, you hear me?"

Nodding her head, she sniffled as the tears continued to fall. Wynner was close as shit with her family; shit, too close, if you asked me. She was the baby out of her two brothers. Wynner was their prized possession, and they all acted like she was glass, and *I* was the bull in the china closet. If they knew that we were at the courthouse in downtown Manhattan and had just got married, they would be fucked up over it.

"I told you I wanted to wait, babe," she sniffled. "Look at me," she complained.

"What do I always tell you?"

She wiped her face and recited what I always told her. "My name may be Wynner, but *you're* the real winner because *I'm* your prize," she repeated.

"So, why are you tripping?" As she fixed her makeup, I swooped her hand in mine and left the chapel before the next couple came in.

Wynner deserved the best wedding money could buy, and eventually, I wanted to give that to her. She deserved to have everything that she wanted and to have her father walk her down the aisle. Right now, I had to grind to get her that, and I had no problem making that shit happen. Her brothers didn't fuck with me, and that was perfectly fine. A lot of people don't fuck with people, but long as the respect is there, I can deal with that. It killed Wynner that she couldn't have her entire family here today, and I just wanted to make her feel better.

"Is that . . ." Her voice trailed off as a black Suburban pulled up in front the courthouse and her brother Uzi hopped out. It didn't matter that it was the afternoon traffic and horns were blowing because he decided to stop traffic.

"Don't tell me you did what the fuck you did!" he barked as I stood with my hands in my pockets. Uzi scared everybody in the streets—except me.

This man was a man like me and bled the same way I did. He wasn't invincible and damn sure wasn't flying around this bitch like a superhero, so why the fuck should I fear him?

"Uzi, right now isn't the time or place," Wynner said, jumping in front of me like she was trying to protect me from him.

"What the fuck do you mean this isn't the time or place, Wyn? You were supposed to be home or some shit," he complained and pulled her by the arm.

Snatching her arm back, she stared at him with tears in her eyes. "I love Qua, Parrish. If you can't respect that, then you don't respect me."

Uzi didn't give a shit about all that she had said. He grabbed ahold of her arm again and dragged her down a few steps. "Wynner, you're 20 years old. What the fuck you know about love? This nigga *my* fucking age," he barked toward me.

Stepping forward, I was about to address the situation, but Wynner's eyes told me otherwise. She was practically begging me to step back. "The heart knows what the heart wants. Let me ask you something, Uzi."

"Nigga, you can't ask me shit, but go ahead."

"Have you ever heard me out here doing wrong on your sister's name? Has she ever came home crying to you or all y'all's mother? Or has she been happy since we been together? I don't have money, cars, and diamonds, but I know damn well I'm gonna die trying to give it to her."

"Baby, you don't have to give me all those things." Wynner tried to pull away from her brother, but his grip was too tight.

"The hell he does. How about you tell me that when I'm footing that thousand-dollar shopping bill every week." He looked down at her. "You don't have family, Qua, so you wouldn't understand. She's my little sis, and I can't just hand her off to you."

"I'm *not* your property," Wynner raised her voice. "All of you think of me as some small piece of property when I'm a woman and capable of making my own decisions. In fact, I made my own decision this morning and married the love of my life."

If looks could kill, Uzi would have pulled out the gun on me I knew was tucked in the back of his jeans and pulled the trigger. "I'm not even trying to hear none of that." He pulled her down the steps toward his truck.

"Nah, you no—"
"Babe, I'll call you tonight," Wynner called back to me.

What had me so tight was the fact that Uzi felt he could just do what he pleased, and I was supposed to be cool. Jahquel, Wynner's other brother, wasn't too bad. He usually minded his own business unless Wynner needed him. It was Uzi who felt the need to step in and run her life. I had hustled enough money to rent a hotel room to be together tonight. Wynner and I had never fucked because she was a virgin. Never being the type to pressure a chick for pussy, we just vibed. We kissed, and I ate her pussy a few times, but nothing more, and I was cool with that. When you met a chick that was the one, pussy was the last thing you were thinking about. Wynner was more than fucking; she did something to me as a person. She made me a better person in the year since I'd met her. Who would have thought I would meet the love of my life at a pizzeria?

Watching my wife be driven away, I shoved my hands into my pockets and started the walk to the train station a few blocks down. One day, I was going to bring in enough money where Wynner wouldn't have to worry about how I was going to eat. Shit, *I* would be the one feeding *her* lobster, steaks, and all that expensive shit. My wife was going to walk around with thousand-dollar bags, shoes, and clothes. She was going to have a nice whip with a big house that I was going to provide for her. Right now, I was down on money and couldn't give her all those things except my promise. Still, Wynner didn't need or want any of that and told me that all the time. All she wanted was me, a nigga that's 27 and still struggling on the block. For that loyalty, I was going to pay her back tenfold . . . Y'all just watch.

Remi

Five Years Later . . .

"Mama, wake up!" I hollered as I pushed her up. "It's not even three in the afternoon and you're high," I complained.

She made some gurgling noise, then slumped over to the opposite side. Pushing her legs out of my path, I walked to the kitchen and made a pot of coffee. I was irritated because I had to be at work at the hospital in half an hour, and I was running superlate. Last night, I spent the entire night working at my night job as a bartender. These late nights and early mornings were going to be the death of me. Then, I had to deal with coming home to my mama high out of her mind and then wake up to the same thing.

"Evelyn, you better go down to the Social Security office and find out why they stopped your damn checks. The rent is due next week, and I'm not covering you again this month. The fuck you think? I'm made out of money?"

My mother moaned and groaned as she waved me off and got more comfortable on the couch. "Quit all that damn yelling, Remi," she grumbled.

My mother was the best mother growing up. Whatever we wanted, she tried to give us. One thing for certain was that we didn't go to bed hungry or dirty. When I was 6, my mother used to weigh over 400 pounds. She could barely move around to tend to me and my sister, yet she did her best, and we never went without. After years, she finally decided to have surgery, and something went wrong. As a child, I couldn't understand why my mother had to stay in the hospital for months while my sister and I had to live between my grandmother and father's house. When she did come out, she was half the size before she went in. Then, she had to start taking all these pills.

In my opinion, that's when life went from sugar to shit. For a while, she was in control of her pills . . . until I hit around 16. Then, she was no longer taking them to relieve pain; she was now abusing them. There was nothing my sister or I could do, especially when she stopped working and started collecting Social Security and food stamps. She completely let herself go and was only concerned about her pills. Now, all she did was abuse her pills, food shop when I forced her to, and run the streets all night. Still, I loved my mother and always wanted her to get better. My sister, Tweeti, was the opposite.

"Ma, I'm serious. You gonna get put out."

"How you gonna put me out of my own shit? My name on the damn lease too. I'll have the damn money, Remi. Now, shut the hell up!" She stood up as best she could and then stumbled down the hall to her bedroom.

Rolling my eyes, I went to shower and change into my scrubs. For the past five years, I've been working at Staten Island Hospital as a personal care assistant. I hated the job; yet, it paid me money to afford my bills and some extra pocket change. At night, I had to travel all the way to Harlem, where I worked at a strip club as a bartender. A few months ago, I considered asking Joey, my manager, to let me get on that damn pole. Money was always tight; still, I made it work. Soon as I was finished getting dressed, I saw the time and sighed. I just knew that I was going to be written up. Peeking into my mother's room, she was lying across her bed snoozing. If there was one thing that mother still did, it was clean. She was an obsessed neat freak, so the apartment was always clean.

"I'm heading out. . . . See you tomorrow," I told her.

"Tomorrow? Why tomorrow?" her voice was muffled as she spoke into her pillow.

"Because I'll be at the club tonight and will probably crash at my coworker's house." Since it was Friday, the club was open even later. I was determined to get all my tips in for the night.

"All right," was all she said.

Before heading out, I knocked on my younger sister Tweeti's door. I didn't expect her to be home, but I knocked and yelled out to her anyway. "See you later, Tweet."

There was no way I was going to make it to work by the bus. With the way the buses were running, I would be late by an hour. By the time I made it downstairs, the cab I had ordered was outside waiting. Hopping inside, I immediately requested that he turn the heat on a bit. It was only the beginning of September, yet it felt like fall was coming in quicker than the summer did. The one thing I loved about the fall was that my birthday was in October. This year, I was turning 26 and couldn't believe I had made it this far without getting knocked up or stuck with a nigga that couldn't offer me shit. Don't get me wrong, I did have relationships that were a waste of time. But I cut them the fuck off soon as I saw they weren't going anywhere.

Right now, I was single and enjoying it. All I was worried about was working and continuing to save my money. A man was nice. Yet, these fools messed around too much for me. They wanted a chick to be faithful, give them good sex, then turn around and give us a piece of dick. Yes, *a piece,* because the dick I've experienced wasn't enough to even make me come. Usually, I had to go into the bathroom and finish the job my damn self. I messed around with this one dude, and we linked up when I felt like being bothered. He called me his girlfriend, even though I didn't claim him. Shaq was the type of dude that you just fucked, rolled up with, and then got rid of him for the rest of the week. He wanted to be in a relationship with me so badly, and I declined each time he brought it up. Shaq had three kids, and the last time I checked, I didn't want to be a stepmama to nobody's kids. He also sold drugs, and I'm not talking about bricks. The nigga sold nickel-and-dime bags, and the weed was trash.

Soon as I walked through the automatic doors of the hospital, my name was called. Quickly rushing to the back to put my bags down, I avoided the manager on shift like the plague. When I turned the corner, she had finally stopped following me. The last thing I needed this morning was a lecture. Shoving my bag into my locker, I took some gum and headed out of the locker room. Grabbing a chart off the first door I passed, I busied myself as if I had been here the whole time.

"Oh no, heifer." Lucy, one of the nurses, grabbed the clipboard from me. "Now, you know damn well you have no business in these charts. You hiding from the manager, aren't you?"

Laughing, I leaned on the nurse's desk and nodded my head. "I had a shitty morning and really need her not to be on my case. Last night, I worked and got home super early this morning."

"Remi, when are you going to quit that bartending job? You said it was just for the summer, and here you are, still working there."

"The tips are good, and it's fun working there."

"Well, how much fun are you having right now?" she questioned as she placed the clipboard back on the patient's door. "You promised me you were going to go to nursing school. What happened to that?"

"It's not what I want to do, Lucy. I tried to look over those books you lent me, and it's not me."

"The club ain't where you should wanna be either, baby doll." She smacked her gum and checked her pager. "Look, it's my treat for lunch today, so see you then?"

"Yep. You need me to do vitals on anyone?"

"Matter of fact, I do. Can you do the whole left side? Whoever's on shift has been slacking this morning, and I have none for any of those patients over on that side."

"I got you."

Lucy was a spitfire Latina nurse that I had gotten cool with. She wasn't like every other nurse in this place who was married to an Italian juicehead with a princess cut diamond engagement ring and drove a damn Maxima. They all turned their noses up at me because I knew their jobs better than they did . . . which is why Lucy was pushing me to go to nursing school. It seemed cool at the time. Then, I thought of all the schooling I had to do, and right now, I needed money. The job at the bar was supposed to be a summer gig. Yet, it was turning out to be much more. The tips and pay were better than here, and with the check from here combined, I was able to pay bills and treat myself every once in a while. With my mother's unreliable ass, I had to be sure I had money to cover both of our asses at the end of the month.

Putting my headphones on, I pushed the electronic blood pressure machine and made my rounds. Tonight, I have to make my way to Harlem to work at the bar, so I needed to get my job done quickly so nobody would try to hold me back once it was time to clock out.

Having a nigga catcall me every other block was super-annoying. Still, I continued until I made it to the club. My favorite bouncer was standing outside, smoking a Black & Mild. When he laid his eyes on me, he blew smoke in the opposite direction, then extended his arms to hug me.

"Didn't I tell you about smoking, Kal?"

He chuckled, then put the cigar out. "And what did I tell you about trying to be my mama?" he asked back.

"Touché . . . What's it looking like in there?" It was a little after eleven by the time I traveled from Staten Island to Harlem. I was running ten minutes behind, and my manager was going to be on my ass. Exotics was one of the most popping and popular clubs in the city. Everybody came there when they were in town. Not to mention, if you were looking for a baller, you could always be certain one would be rolling through with his squad.

"Packed, and it's been open for only an hour. Joey came out here looking for you like five minutes ago. The bar is packed as hell."

"I'm only ten minutes late . . . He's always dragging it."

"You know you're one of the best bartenders he has . . . get in there and get to work." He shoved me inside.

Walking through, everyone was surrounding the bar, trying to get their drink order put in before heading to their sections. Slipping to the back, I quickly changed into the skintight latex shorts and red crop top while lacing up my heels. Even though I didn't strip, the outfits that were mandated to wear were close to the ones the strippers wore. I never complained since my body was a work of art, literally. I had tattoos all over my body, and they were my pride and joy.

Just as I was coming out the back, I ran right into Joey, who had his cell phone gripped in his hands. If I had to guess, he was probably dialing my number and leaving me a million voicemails.

"Rem, where did you come from? I've been calling your phone for the past three hours." He jumped down my throat.

Real nonchalant, I messed with my box braids and fixed myself further before going behind the bar. "You're superannoying, Joey. You know that? Nigga, you know I have another job, so why the hell would you be calling me for three hours?"

"Because I needed you here earlier. I would have paid for an Uber for you."

"Oh, and compensated me for lost hours at my other job too?" His face told me all I needed to know. "Exactly. I'm ten minutes late past my regular hours. You're holding me up with this pointless talk."

"You keep forgetting that I'm your boss," he reminded me like he reminded me every time I came at him.

"And you keep forgetting that damn near every strip club in the city wants me behind their bar. The reason I stay is because I'm loyal, and you were the only person who took a chance on me. However, don't get it twisted and think I won't go somewhere else and get more money."

"Whatever, Remi. Get behind the bar," he mumbled and headed to the dressing room.

Joey knew damn near every strip club wanted me behind their bar. I brought my own customers to the bar by announcing when I was working on my social media accounts. He refused to pay me more, and I never complained. Yet, when his ass needed me, he had no problem calling me in. Going behind the bar, I walked right into chaos. Instead of promoting me to head bartender, where I could actually train these dumb asses he hired, he'd rather put me right behind the bar, where they made my job harder.

"Move. He doesn't want a virgin drink; give him more liquor," I coached her.

"That's more like it. How you doing, Remi?" one of my regulars greeted me. "Shorty been giving me watered drinks since I walked in here an hour ago."

"Well, I'm here now, and we won't have those problems anymore. I'm doing good, babe." I snatched the bottle of liquor from her and poured more into his drink before sliding it over to him.

"I know you're good . . . just by looking at you." He winked, slid a twenty on the bar, and headed off to get his front seat while waiting for the girls to hit the stage.

"Why do you always do that?" Trish complained.

"Bitch, you know that damn twenty wasn't for you. Especially not with that baby shot you were giving him."

"Still, that was *my* customer, and you took *my* tip," she continued to complain while I shoved the twenty into my bra.

"Trish, you wanna sit here and complain, then move to the side. I have bills and don't have time to be listening to you crying." She began to say something, but I walked off and started getting all these people away from my counter.

Joey liked them all seated when the girls came out, so the faster I got them away from this bar, the better it was for me. Then, I could count my money until the next rush came, and I collected even more tips. While I got everyone their drink orders and moved them away from my bar, Trish went to the back to complain to Joey. I knew he didn't care what she said because he just needed me to do my job so the owners weren't on *his* ass.

"Hey, baby doll, hit me with one before I go on stage." Lexi, one of the strippers, tapped the bar. She was always asking for a double shot before she went on and did her thing.

Grabbing the Cîroc, I poured it into the shot glass and slid it over to her. "One of those nights already?"

"Yes, and then Joey wants me to work the private rooms after my set." She rolled her eyes and took her shot down.

"Can I crash at your place tonight?"

Signaling for another shot, I slid it across the table, and she gulped it down. "Yeah, you know you're welcomed. Come get my keys when you're done with your shift. I'll be home late," she explained and walked off toward the back.

The lights lowered, and the music started. Men were roaring and whistling as they anticipated what dancer would come out first. Sitting on the bar stool, I counted up the tips I had accumulated over the short amount of time I'd been there. A hundred dollars wasn't bad for being here for less than twenty minutes.

"Rem, stop taking Trish's tips," Joey whispered in my ear as he started making himself a drink.

"Joe, I'm not even going there with you. When you hired her, did you fuck? 'Cause that bitch don't know how to do anything."

He chuckled. "Nah, her pops is a good friend of mine. Teach her instead of trying to do everything and take her tips."

Stuffing my money into my bra, I stared at him like he had lost his mind. "Pay me more then. Because last I checked, my job was to bartend, *not* play teacher."

"We can arrange that," he promised as he took his drink to the head.

"Soon as you arrange that and we sign on it, *then* I'll start."

"Damn, you need to sign on it?"

"Yep."

Once Joey got from behind the bar, I focused on the stage, where one of the dancers was shaking her ass like it had a mind of its own. A few times, I thought about climbing on the stage and doing my thing. Then, I thought about all these men tossing money at me and seeing my whole body and talked myself out of it.

"Aye, let me get some Henny on the rocks, and then give me the whole bottle," a voice demanded behind me.

My first instinct was to be pissed since I wasn't behind the bar, and everyone knew if I wasn't behind the bar, then I was taking a small break. It didn't matter that I had just walked in twenty minutes ago; all that mattered was that I managed to get everyone their drinks by myself while Trish stood there and complained about me taking her little stupid tip. My feet were already hurting, and I hadn't been here a full hour. So, whoever it was that was requesting me to step behind the bar better be tipping me fifty dollars or more.

"Who the . . ." My voice trailed off when my eyes took a look at this beautiful man standing in front of me.

His caramel skin was glistening like he had just got a damn facial before he walked into the club. Then, his lips . . . Man, his lips were so juicy that I almost lost sight of his pearly whites that were perfectly aligned with one another. On the bottom, he had gold grills in and kept licking his lips, which turned me on more and more. His eyes were chinky, so while he smirked, it appeared that they were closed, but they were just really low as if he took a good pull of some weed. Baby's nose was on the big side; still, it fit perfectly in the center of his face. He had to be a good six feet and couldn't weigh no more than a hundred and fifty pounds. He wasn't fit with a hard-rock stomach and chiseled abs, but from his shirt, I could tell he enjoyed a good meal every once in a while.

"Damn, you gonna continue to stare at me or get what the fuck I asked for?" I knew it was all too good to be true. Was a fine man that was a gentleman too much to ask for, God?

"You have two options." He leaned forward slightly so he could hear me over the music. "One, you can wait until I get behind the bar, or two, you can go across the street and get your drink, then pay to get the fuck back in here. Talking to me like that, you ain't even all that," I lied, knowing damn well he *was* all of that *and* a bag of salt and vinegar chips.

Laughing, he leaned on the counter like he was trying to study me. "How long you been working here?"

"Don't matter."

"If there's one thing I can't stand, it's a woman with a slick-ass mouth," he told me like I gave a shit.

"If it's one thing that I can't stand, it's a man with no manners that don't know how to take no for an answer."

"That's two things," he insisted on pointing out.

"Glad to see that you know how to count. It would be a pity if you were dumb as you look." Sitting up, I went behind the bar and poured myself a shot of liquor and took it to the head.

Mystery man then took a seat on the stool and continued to stare at me, which was making me nervous. There was something about the way he was staring at me that made me want to tell him how I dared my sister to steal gum out of the corner store when we were younger.

"What, nigga?" I slapped my hand on the counter hard. The stinging on my hand was killing me; still, I stayed with a brave and pissed-off facial expression.

"My drink," he calmly requested for the second time.

Mumbling, I turned around and made his dumb-ass drink so he could leave my bar. For a man so damn fine, he sure did piss me off that quick. "Here, and you need to pay for the bottle before I allow you to take it."

Nodding his head, he pulled out a hundred-dollar bill, then handed it to me. "That should cover me."

"Let me go get your change." I reached across the table and grabbed the money. As I was about to turn, he grabbed my arm gently.

"Nah, that's your tip."

"You're tipping me?"

He took his drink back with one gulp. "You surprised?"

"I am, but then again, I'm not, because I'm probably the most entertainment you've had all day."

"Yeah, you right about that. Hit me again." He pushed his cup out, and I poured more into it. His smirk had faded to a deep scowl as he thought about something.

"Wanna talk about it? I'm always the person who's giving advice behind this bar. These other hoes are dumb."

He laughed when the words left my mouth. "Damn, you harsh."

"Shit, you will see for yourself. Try me out."

"Nah, this too much for anybody. What's your name?"

"Remi. Who wants to know?"

"Uzi," he replied nonchalantly.

"Your mama did not name you that, so what's your *real* name?"

He requested me to pour him some more, then opened his mouth but closed it when one of the strippers came up to him. "What you doing over here, babe? I got you your own section for me and you tonight." Kandle rubbed her hand all on his shoulders.

Kandle was a straight ho and fucked any nigga that walked into this club. A few times, I caught her and Joey fucking in his office. It didn't matter who she fucked;

she just wanted dick and whatever money they provided after. This bitch and I didn't have beef; yet, she knew I disliked her, and we didn't speak unless it had something to do with work.

"Yeah, I'm chilling right now." He removed her hands from around his neck. "Shouldn't you be working?"

"Yes, daddy. I just want to feel you inside me," she cooed, which caused me to choke. For the first time since she sauntered her ass over here, she noticed that I was standing here. "You got a cold? What you coughing for?"

"Kandle, you and I both know that I'll wax your ass all through this club with no remorse. Let's not forget or try to act cute." With that, I turned on my heels and went to the other side of the bar to continue working.

Uzi must have liked whatever Kandle was spitting in his ear for the ten minutes she stood there because he nodded toward me and took the bottle to the area she reserved for him. The entire night, I worked behind the bar and was raking in so many tips. It got so out of hand that I even called Trish behind the bar to teach her how to make drinks the right way. She was all too hype when I split a hundred-dollar tip with her ass.

At closing time, there were always a few strippers who stayed behind to hang with whatever baller requested their presence for the night. It was no surprise when Lexi came over to me with a smile on her face. I just knew she had something to tell me from the way she kept batting her eyelashes at me like she wanted to fuck me instead.

"What now, Lexi?" I was banking on staying at her house tonight. The last thing I wanted to do was travel home at this hour. The degrees had gone down, and I'd be standing at the bus stop freezing cold.

"I met some dude, and he has money, Remi. Take my keys and make yourself at home. I'll call you tomorrow and let you know if I'll be home." She giggled as she tossed her keys across the bar and quickly ran to the back.

A part of me wanted to be happy that I didn't have to travel back to Staten Island tonight; then the other half of me was pissed because Lexi had a car and could have driven us to her apartment. Stuffing the keys in the pockets of my shorts, I continued to clean the bar so I could take my ass to her apartment and sleep. After working two jobs, I was tired as hell and needed a few hours of sleep before heading back to Staten Island in the morning.

Tweeti

"Sundae, I asked you to make me look like damn Beyoncé, not fucking Panky, nugga," I mocked the actor from the popular movie *Friday*.

Here I was, thinking that my hair was about to be all of that *and* a bag of chips, but when this bitch spun me around, I wanted to kick her in the damn throat. Why did I think that supporting my neighbor across the hall was a good idea? Here she was, standing here all emotional like *she* was the one with the fucking Jheri curl.

"Sundae, tell me what you did exactly," I demanded.

When this bitch showed me the bottle of white people perm, I wanted to cry. I thought she was washing my hair, and this bitch was adding chemicals into my hair to make it look like Bobby Sue from West Virginia who bartends when she's not with her twelve cats in a one-bedroom apartment. I may be dragging it, yet I was pissed that I had to walk around like this until this shit wore off—or however you got rid of it.

"I'm so sorry, Tweeti." Her voice cracked as she was about to break down. "I saw my classmate do it, and it came out real nice."

"Oh yeah? So did she look like Eazy-E or Ice Cube when she was done?"

"Let me fix it." She tried to touch my hair, but I dodged away from her ass.

"You lucky I don't beat your little ass. I got your card, though. Watch me come back and toss some hot shit at your door." Sitting up, I grabbed my purse and walked across the hall to my apartment. I shouldn't have been all that mad at Sundae because I knew she was fresh out of beauty school. Still, I trusted that she could at least wash my damn hair and then put some curls in it.

When I walked through the door, my mama was sitting on the couch, eating chips and washing it down with soda. You would think that after she had surgery years ago that she would eat the right way. Nope. She continued to eat how she did before the surgery. Lucky for me, I had got hit with the fat stick while my older sister, Remi, was hit with the nice and thick stick. All my life, I was told that I needed to stop eating this, or I needed to start running. A bunch of bullshit, if you asked me, because I did all they asked, and I'm still a big, beautiful woman. My mother was the opposite. She felt like I should get the same surgery she had, which was out of the question. It would be one thing if I wasn't healthy; however, I watched what I ate, made smart choices, and checked in with my doctor regularly.

"Why the hell you walking in here looking like Little Richard?" my mother smacked on some chips and questioned.

"Fuck you, Evelyn," I shot back and continued to my bedroom. As I made my way to my bedroom, I could hear her laughing like this shit was funny.

My mother's and my relationship was strained, and she knew it. While some kids had to be put into foster care, Remi and I had our father and grandmother who guided us and made sure we were all right. My mother cared too much about her pills and how she could get more once she ran out. So, when it came to teaching me about things that I needed to know, she wasn't there. Or, should I say, she was there and was just passed out or too high to teach me. Remi and my mother shared a weird relationship because although she couldn't stand our mother, she was still nice to her. Me, I called her by her real name because she didn't deserve to be called Mom. All my memories of her were picking her up off the floor or telling her to pull her head out of the freezer because she had fallen asleep in it again.

Slamming my bedroom door closed, I plopped down onto my bed and sighed. My hair looked like a curly-ass mess, and then I had to worry about how I was going to see my boo and get my rent money from him. Growing up, these boys loved to tell me how pretty I was for a big girl. Then, there were the ones who liked to bully me and make me feel like shit. It was funny how those same niggas were now calling my phone to chill with my big ass. Relationships weren't for me, so, I'd rather let a nigga think that's what we had until he handed me the things I wanted. Remi told me that I was heartless because I did this, but I called it being paid as fuck. Well, not all that paid because I was still living at home and barely holding up my end of the rent with these unreliable-ass niggas.

Grabbing my phone, I dialed Oaks, one of the dudes I was talking to. He had me feeling like he could be the one; yet, I was still waiting for him to fuck up.

"Yo, what's good, ma?"

"Hey, I'm good. What you 'bout to get into?"

"Shit, I'm chilling at the crib bored as fuck. My nigga 'bout to come home and put some steaks on the grill."

"Oh yeah? When are we going to link up?"

"Shit, I can come scoop you now, and we can chill," he suggested.

The steaks he had mentioned sounded good, but I didn't want to sit around making small talk. Oaks was cool, so I was considering not following a page from my own book with him. Just as I was about to tell him that he could come scoop me, I caught a glimpse of my damn hair and changed my mind quickly.

"I have a bunch of things to do right now. Can we link tomorrow?"

"No doubt. Stay beautiful, baby," he told me, and we ended the call.

I had half a mind to go over to Sundae's mama's door and smear shit all over the door handle. She had me walking around looking like Little Orphan Annie. My money was low, so there was no way I would be able to go to the salon, pay rent, *and* keep a little money in my pocket. When I was younger, I had this whole plan on how things were going to turn out for me. I was going to go to college, meet my future husband, get married, and then have his little babies. All of that was still on my list, except I wanted my nigga to have bank and treat me like a plush queen. Well, maybe I didn't want any kids right now, but I did want to meet the one that would change my thoughts on men.

"Tweet, what the hell?" Remi burst out laughing as she swung her bag on her door handle. "What did you let Sundae do to you now?"

"When will I learn, right?"

"Exactly. That girl barely passed beauty school by the skin of her teeth. Let me see what I can do." Remi came in and started running her hands through my hair. "Just cut, sis."

"Cut it? I love all my hair. I'll walk around looking like Rick James for a few weeks."

Remi was a jack-of-all-trades. She could take your blood pressure, do your hair, and fix you a good-ass drink. Why she never took up cosmetology was beyond me.

"I know you love it. You've been saying you want a different look forever. Just let me hook you up, I promise."

Sighing, I nodded my head. "Have me looking like a damn rat and I'll shave your eyebrow in your sleep."

"Come to my room in like ten minutes. I wanna roll up and get blazed before doing your hair," she told me like I was going to be cool with this shit.

"Rem, I love you and all, but you're not going to be high as fuck cutting my damn hair."

"Fine," she finally agreed.

Remi did her own hair and always slayed the shit out of it, so I wasn't worried about her messing my hair up. Walking into her room, she unpacked her work bag and turned her radio on as she hummed to an old Janet Jackson song.

"How was work last night? Made any tips?"

"Girl, you know I did. That's the only reason I agreed to come in, in the first place. Trish was even able to get a little piece of change too."

"She still work there? That bitch is so damn stupid."

"Who you telling? Joey wants me to train her, but ain't talking about raising my pay. I helped her out and taught her some shit last night because it was only me, but I ain't teaching her shit else."

Once Remi unpacked her bag, showered, and located her hair bag, she got to work on my hair as we talked. Although she was older than me by two years, we were so tight that you would have thought we were the same age. Well, some thought I was older than Remi, but she was the oldest. My sister was my entire world, and I would move mountains if she asked me to. Bitches these days were fake, and I didn't know who to trust. If there was one thing I could count on, it was my sister.

"Who you fucking now?" she bluntly asked.

"Nobody. I've been trying to link with Oaks, but we both been busy. We're supposed to link soon."

Oaks was a nigga I met when I was heading uptown
to get my hair braided. He was chilling in front of the
grocery store near the salon. One look at me, and I knew
he wanted to talk to me. Like a hawk on its prey, he followed me down the block and asked me for my number.
He was cute, so I gave him my number, and we've been
talking ever since. It had been hard to link since I lived in
Staten Island, and he was from Harlem. He claimed that
his friend been holding his car down. I believed the nigga
didn't have a car and didn't want to admit the shit to me.
All I asked was for a man to keep it real with me. If you
didn't have a car, that was cool with me.

"Oh, homie from Harlem? Y'all still haven't linked up?
What y'all waiting on?" she continued to clip my precious
hair and ask a million questions.

Staring at my hair on the floor, I decided to focus on
the questions instead. "He claims his friend been using
his car a lot."

"He don't have a damn car. Why niggas gotta always
lie?"

"My point exactly. That nigga always bragging about
the type of money he has, so I wanna see how much he
peel off for me when we do meet."

"Tweet, you know I can get you a job at the bar, right?"

"That's not what I wanna do. Working in a bar is your
thing."

"What exactly *is* your thing? Every job you get, you quit
because you hate it. Like, what do you really wanna do,
sis?"

"Rem, you think if I knew that I wouldn't be doing it
right now? Every job seems cool when I start, and then I
don't care about it anymore. I should just be a hustler's
wife, for real."

"There are consequences to having that nice and lavish
lifestyle. Being the wife of a street king ain't all that it's
cracked up to be."

"How would you know? Shaq's ass ain't nowhere near street king status."

"Oh, hell nah. His ass can't even sell bomb weed, so I know he ain't no damn street king. I'm just saying, Tweet. It's nice to have your own instead of letting a man provide that for you."

"All that sound nic—"

"But you're going to do what you're going to do," she finished my sentence.

The one thing that set me and Remi apart was our personalities. We were both outgoing and quick with the mouth. The one thing that made us different was Remi's drive to hustle and get the things she wanted. She had been working since she was 16 and hadn't stopped yet. Me, working wasn't for me, and I couldn't see myself sitting behind someone's desk punching keyboard keys for minimum wage. Each time I tried, it always failed, and I was gone before lunchtime. It wasn't that I wanted a man to take care of me, 'cause that was only half true. I just wanted a career that made me want to get out of the bed and work.

"Anyway, what's been going on with you?"

"Work, work, and some more work. I really need a night out or something."

"You work tonight?"

"No, but I'm too tired to put on a tight dress, heels, and act like I'm interested in conversation for a free drink."

"I feel you. After Sundae's bullshit, I think I'm gonna chill in the house today too. Mama leaving soon?"

Remi laughed. "Yes, she's going to the Poconos with her little friend. Wonder how he's going to take it when she shows him the *real* her."

"She won't be seeing him no more. It's crazy because he's the nicest man ever, and she's going to fuck it up."

Evelyn started dating this man that she had met. He had actually found the wallet she lost and returned it. Eddie was the sweetest man with traits handpicked by God. He worked an honest job as an MTA worker during the day, and at night, he would come here to take my mother wherever she wanted. When it was too late, he would stay over, and they would be freaks in the next room. One time, he told me that he knew my mother was the woman he was supposed to marry and wanted to ask for her hand in marriage. As I was about to tell him about my mother's ugly prescription pill problem, Remi cut me off and told him to wait awhile longer. That was six months ago, and I knew he was going to ask her this weekend when he took her out.

"He's such a sweet man, and he loves Mommy . . ." Remi sighed as her voice trailed off.

"You should have let me tell him what she was about, Rem. We're just as bad as she is." The issue I had with my mother was plain and simple: her drug addiction. Although we never went without food or no crazy shit like that, an addiction was an addiction. It didn't matter how well you managed it.

My mother was usually high at night when it was time to abuse her night medicine. She claimed she had insomnia and told her doctor she could never sleep. After seeing this for so long, I knew she had no damn insomnia and just wanted the pills. Not to mention, she complained about this fake pain in her leg so she could continue to receive Percocets. All she had to do was get clean and prove to me that she should be called Mom. Yes, she was there with advice when we needed it, but half the time, she really needed to be taking the advice she gave us. She and my father didn't work out because he wanted different things than she wanted. My father wanted to move out of the projects, buy a home, and have a son—all things that my mother *didn't* want at all.

They didn't get along now and would rather talk shit about the other than have a cordial relationship for Remi and me. The thing that bothered me the most about my mother was that Eddie was a good man. A good man that didn't deserve her; yet, he wanted her in the worst way. There was nothing more heartwarming than a man wanting you so badly that he'd accept every part of you. Most days, my mother didn't brush or comb her hair; yet, Eddie didn't mind and still called her beautiful anyway.

"Done," Remi smiled and handed me her handheld mirror.

Staring into the mirror, I winked my eye at myself with a huge smirk on my face. Do you know how many niggas I was about to pull with this short pixie cut? "I don't even need to say it because you know what I'm going to say."

"Still, I like to hear you say it," she giggled and started cleaning the hair on the floor. "I'm waiting."

"You're a beast with the clippers, and I love my hair."

"And?"

"And, you're so damn fine, and I wanna name my first child after you."

"Thank you," she laughed. "Now, leave so I can clean and sleep."

"Can you color it blond tomorrow?"

"Bih, do you think this a full-service salon? Fine. Go get all I need, because I ain't paying for nothing."

"All right."

My hair was still slightly curly, but with a good blow dry, this baby would be nice and straight. Closing her room door, I went into my bedroom and lay down across my bed. I wasn't sleepy, but I decided to turn on the TV to catch up on some shows. Today was going to be an in-the-house type of day. Plus, I needed all my energy to whip Sundae's ass tomorrow when I saw her.

Uzi

As I sat in the hospital room visiting my sister, I scrolled over the text message with Remi's number. My nigga, Joey, had hooked me up with her cell phone number because I asked about her. By the time I finished with Kandle's smut ass in the private room, the bar was closed, and she was ghost. When I asked where she went, all the strippers said that she didn't play when it came to her time to clock out. Kandle was being all clingy like we were something more than fuck buddies. I allowed her to suck my dick in the private room, then dipped to find Remi. Kandle was being a hater, like she didn't want to tell me Remi's phone number, so I asked another stripper, who happened to be Lexi. She explained that Remi was staying at her apartment and going home in the morning. Truth be told, she gave too much information about shorty, yet I took it all in my mental Rolodex.

"You know you can go home, Parrish." My sister smiled as she wiped the sleep out of her eyes.

Wynner was my heart, soul, and entire life. She was the baby out of both me and my brother, Jahquel. We spoiled her; yet, we were real protective over her too. When she married her husband, Qua, I was pissed as fuck. That nigga didn't have the respect to have my parents or us there, so why should I respect him? It was all because of Wynner that I had decided to put our differences aside. I was robbed of seeing my baby sister get married, and he could never fix that in my eyes.

"Nah, I wanna spend time with you . . . How you feeling?"

"Ah, I'm here, ain't I?" she joked like the shit was funny to me.

Wynner was diagnosed with lupus two years ago. When we found out, I dropped to my knees and prayed it away. Why couldn't it be given to me, or someone else? I knew it was a fucked-up thought, but when it came to Wynner, I just wanted to protect her all the time. This disease was so draining on her body that she was either sick or in and out of the hospital all the time. Like now, she had been in the hospital for a few days and was set to be released tomorrow. I knew she hated being in the hospital instead of doing shit like normal 25 year olds.

"Stop doing that shit, Wyn."

"Parrish, why are you so uptight? I want to laugh, smile, and joke. Is that so bad?"

"No, it's not that bad. Except you keep doing joking when it comes to your health. Where's Qua?"

"He told me that he had to make a run for you and Jah. He'll be back later on tonight," she explained her husband's absence.

I could do two things when I found out they went and got married. One, I could hold a grudge and cut my sister off, or two, I could put my new brother-in-law on so he could take care of my baby sister. Ever since I put him on, they stayed in a nice high-rise condo in the city, Wynner had a closet filled with designer clothes, and he had replaced that small-ass ring with a huge rock on her finger. I wished I could front like I had to make him do all those things; yet, I didn't. Soon as he started breaking bread with me, all his money went to making sure Wynner had a place they could call home. For the first year of their marriage, Wynner still lived home with my parents, and he lived wherever he stayed at.

Once the money rolled in, he went and put a down payment on a nice-ass condo in Greenwich Village and made sure she didn't want for anything. My sister had everything at her fingertips. If Qua couldn't provide it, Jah or I would give it to her. Not to mention, our parents had her spoiled since she was the only girl. Our entire world revolved around Wynner. When she was younger, she ate this shit up and played into being the spoiled princess. As she got older, and now that she had a husband, she couldn't stand how involved we wanted to be in her life. My parents were waiting for a grandchild, but that shit wasn't going to happen just yet. My sis was only 25 and didn't need a baby right now. Qua was 31 and had lived his life. Now, it was time for Wynner to live hers. I had the nigga by a year, so I, myself, knew he was too damn old for my baby sister.

"Yo, Wyn, let me ask you something."

"Shoot." She sat up in the bed, glad to be talking about anything else besides herself.

"I met shorty at the bar yesterday and got her number from the manager. Me and him go way back, so he slid me the digits. Would I look like a stalker if I hit her up?"

"Yes, but since when you care about what you look like?"

"Yeah, you right. Let me go call this little honey dip, 'cause she fine as fuck." As the flashbacks of our encounter, last night, ran through my head, I couldn't help but lick my lips at shorty.

Remi was brown-skinned with tattoos everywhere on her body. When I say everywhere, she had them down her leg, across her stomach, and down both of her arms. Usually, I didn't like a woman with more ink than me; yet, she wore that shit well and made my dick hard envisioning her naked. Some people collected paintings, but all I wanted to do was hang Remi somewhere else, and it wasn't on a damn wall. Her lips were so pouty that they resembled little pink clouds when she spoke. Then, her small, pointy nose just added more perfection to her beautiful canvas of a face. Those damn eyes will have any nigga doing whatever she wanted because she batted them at me once, and I was ready to give her the world. Standing at five foot four, she was short as fuck, yet the thickness of her ass, thighs, and breasts made up for the loss of height. I could just pick her short ass up and toss her over my shoulder.

Dialing her number, I placed the phone to my ear and waited for her to answer. When she didn't, I placed my phone in my pocket and prepared to go back into Wynner's room. Suddenly, my pocket buzzed, and there was Ms. Remi, calling me right back. Sliding my finger across the screen, I placed the phone on speaker and leaned up against the wall outside of Wynner's room.

"What's good?"

"What's good? Who the hell is this?" she repeated my words before she went off on who the mysterious caller was.

"Why you going off? Chill and take a breath for a second. I know you were expecting my call."

On her end, I could hear her suck her teeth. "Listen, I'm in the middle of some good-ass sleep and hate when people play on my phone, so either say who you are, or I'm hanging up."

"So, hang up then."

My phone made a beeping sound that indicated that she had hung up on a nigga. The shit was funny because her little attitude and slick mouth did something to me. I loved a woman that could challenge me and wasn't afraid to speak her mind. When it came to women I fucked with, they loved for me to tell them what to do, think, or how to act. The only time they wanted to have a voice was when they found out that they were nothing more than a quick fuck for me. Dialing her number again, I waited until she came back on the line.

"Whaaaaaat?" she screamed.

"Remi, why the hell you screaming in this damn house?" an older woman yelled.

"Mama, leave me alone," Remi huffed, and then I heard a door slam.

From that small bit, I knew she lived with her mother, and that it didn't matter who you were . . . She still had the smart-ass lip. "Aye, don't talk to your mother like that."

"You don't know my life, so stop trying to tell me how to live it. Now, who the fuck is this playing on my phone? The next time, I'm not only going to hang up, but I'm also going to block this number."

"Chill. Why you wanna block my number? I thought we were homies. . . . I mean, you were pouring my drink, and I hooked you up with a nice-ass tip."

"I pour a lot of drinks, and I get hooked up with a lot of tips, so you ain't telling me much."

"Uzi," was all I said, and she started laughing.

"Nigga, you did all of this playing on my phone when you could have told me who you were. How did you get my number anyway?"

"I have ways."

"Tell me about your ways."

"Then, I would have to kill you."

"It'll be worth it. Who gave you my number?" she continued.

"Damn, you wake up on a hundred, huh?"

She giggled into the phone. "Yes, especially when people play on my phone and interrupt my beauty sleep."

"It's five in the evening, the fuck you still doing asleep?"

I knew shorty worked at the club, and she dipped when it closed, but, damn, she that tired that she slept the entire day away? Me, I couldn't sleep past seven in the morning. My body wouldn't let me sleep in, and the only time I did sleep in was when I was battling a hangover from the previous morning.

"Well, I do work another job before heading to the bar. I'm tired as hell, so I'm gonna sleep when I get the chance to. Now, I'm hungry as hell," she muttered to herself.

"You having side conversations and shit?" I pointed out, and she laughed. "What you doing right now?"

"Lying in my twin-sized bed with panties on and trying to debate if I wanna catch a cab down to Popeyes."

"Popeyes? I haven't eaten there in a minute. Twin-sized? How the fuck am I going to lay up with you?"

"Uh-huh, they got this five-dollar box, and I can taste the chicken now. Your ass ain't lying up in my bed. I don't even know you. Anyway, why did you call, *Uzi?*" The way she said my name made my dick rock hard. I could picture her lying in the bed with nothing on except panties.

"If I wanna get up in your bed, trust, I will."

"Answer the question." She ignored me.

"Why else you think?"

Shorty wasn't 'bout to get me to say anything further than that. The name always stuck because the gun I preferred was a damn Uzi. When I first started out in this drug game, I was 16 years old. They showed me guns, and the first one I picked was an Uzi. My big homie was the first to try to call my bluff by making me shoot some nigga that stole from him. Nigga thought I was about to be soft and start acting like a little bitch. I let that Uzi off like a fucking pro, then dropped the shit to the floor and walked off when I was done. The nigga I was only supposed to shoot once was now riddled with holes. Knowing that this nigga stole irritated my entire soul. There were two things I couldn't stand, and that was a thief and a liar. You never knew where you stood with those types of people because they were good at pretending, and that was the fucking shit that I couldn't stand."

"Guess you're going to be vague about it."

I noticed my brother going into the room and figured I needed to wrap shit up with this call. Yet, I wasn't about to wrap the call up until I had some time lined up with her.

"Let me take you out."

"Just bring me a five-dollar box, and we're good. I'm starving."

"Let me take you to Benihana's." She wanted a simple five-dollar meal when I could introduce her to the finer things in life. "Let me take you on a real date."

"You can actually do both. In order to get me on the date with you, however, I need to see you pull up to Staten Island with some Popeyes chicken," she challenged like that eighteen-dollar toll meant shit to me.

"Bet. Let me handle this situation I'm dealing with, and I'll be out there. Text me your address."

"No, we're going to do it on *my* terms. You have an iPhone?"

"Of course. I ain't with that Android shit."

"Facetime me when you're in Popeyes. I'm not about to just hand out my address until I see you're serious."

"Damn, where's the trust?"

"It'll come when you buy that damn chicken. Handle business, and, hopefully, I'll see you in a little bit."

"Bet."

We both ended the call, and I went into Wynner's room, where my brother was questioning her about something. Jah and Wynner had always been closer than she and I. To her, I was the very overly protective older brother, which I was. I wore the title proudly, long as my sister was straight. While all her other little friends ended up being teen mothers to niggas that didn't give a shit about them or the kids they birthed, Wynner was able to finish school and never had to worry about none of that. My mother always lectured me about letting her make her own mistakes, but if I could help her avoid that, then I was going to do that. When I walked into the room, they stopped talking, and Wynner was wiping away tears.

"What you did to her that quickly?"

My brother spun around in his chair and dapped me up. "What the streets saying?" That was the way we greeted each other each time we linked.

"That the McKnights still running shit everywhere." He laughed as our hands clasped together.

"Bet. What's good with you, Wyn?"

"Nothing. I just want to go home." She avoided eye contact with me. I knew she was lying because she could never stare me in the face when she lied. Instead of pressing her on the subject, I turned my attention back to my brother.

"Who drove you up here?"

"Some fine little honey I been fucking with," he chuckled.

Jahquel used to play basketball, football, and soccer. The nigga was in love with sports and played up until high school. We were only two years apart from each other, but everyone called us twins. We moved the same way and acted the same way. Once I was involved in the streets, he got involved and held me down. My pops used to be in the streets back in the day and left that life to bring us up. Every now and then, he got his hands dirty to handle shit for me; yet, that was all it was. When he left the game, he invested his money wisely in a bunch of businesses where he collected money from. When I get that age, I prayed to do the same thing.

"You stay with some little ho," Wynner commented. "When are you both going to settle down?" She did her usually questioning.

I had nothing against settling down with a woman. It was the women that I had to choose from that made me put a stop to those plans. All these bitches wanted was a man to pay their bills and support their shopping. There was nothing wrong with taking care of or even treating my woman, but when she expected the shit, that's when I got turned off. I needed a woman that saw past all the money I had and was down for me because I was a trill-ass nigga with a sense of humor.

"When the right one bring her ass over here. Right now, ain't no chick checking for some crippled nigga in a wheelchair," Jah told her straight up.

"You're an amazing man. It doesn't matter that you're in a wheelchair. That doesn't define you, Jahquel," Wynner continued.

"Yeah, this dick still work, so as long as it's working, I'm gonna slang it around on these bitches that see my money before me."

Shaking her head, she pulled the covers back from her body and sat up. "And, what about you?"

"I'm around. Besides Kandle, I ain't messing with nobody else right now."

Wynner didn't bother to hide her face when I mentioned Kandle's name. The only reason Wynner knew who she was because Kandle kept trying to insert herself into my life. I don't know how many times I've told her to chill the fuck out with that. She would pop up at places she knew I would be at, acting like she "just so happened" to be there. Wynner had met her when we both were having dinner at Olive Garden one night. A nigga could afford the most expensive places, yet there was nothing like restaurants like Olive Garden.

"Yuck, why are you even fucking a stripper in the first place, Parrish?" Wynner and my mother were the only women that called me by my government name.

"'Cause she gives me good head. Do I question why you married Qua?"

"Hell yeah," Qua answered as he walked into the room. Our relationship was shaky; still, we had times when we could kick it, and I would forget he married my little sister without permission.

He walked over to Wynner and kissed her on the forehead before taking a seat on her bed. "*Bam!*" Wynner laughed.

"You damn right I'm 'bout to ask all the damn time. She's my little sister."

"Here he go again," Jah laughed and rolled over to Qua to dap him. Their relationship was better because he and Wynner were so close. I assumed he decided to bury the issues because of Wynner.

"I took care of that, and got the next shit on the trucks on their way down to Atlanta now," Qua informed me.

The reason his ass was alive was that he was smart, loyal, and hardworking. That nigga worked hard as fuck when he didn't need to. He never asked me to allow him to move up the ladder because he was content with the work I gave him. All he did was work, take care of my sister, and stay in the crib with her. He had all the qualities of a man that I should have wanted Wynner with, but I was still pissed about the way he went about things. Yeah, years have passed, but it still pissed me the fuck off.

"Bet. We gotta talk about the shit that's been going on in Harlem."

Harlem was the place where I made the most money. It was crazy how Brooklyn, Queens, Staten Island, and the Bronx came second to Harlem. I had so many people copping out there, and it was mostly because of the white people that came from the Upper East Side to cop pills or meth. I had congressmen coming to me to supply their little meetings with some goodies and, as always, long as the money was right, I would make sure they received their "care packages," as they liked to call them.

"Yeah, I was thinking we need to start being stricter. No offense, but you been letting them punk you out there," Qua voiced his opinion like he always did.

You would think because this nigga was a year younger, married my sister, and knew I didn't particularly like him that he wouldn't have much to say. It was the opposite, however; he always had some shit to say and didn't care that I didn't want to hear from his ass. Wynner gave me the look that told me that I better be on my best behavior. My sister had saved a lot of people, and I bet she didn't even realize that she did.

"How the fuck you think I'm being punked? Nigga, I walk through there and them niggas won't even look me in the face."

"There's a difference between being feared and re-spected. Them niggas fear you and disrespect you when your back is turned. You don't need or want those types of people on your team. I mean, you gonna do what you wanna do, so you could continue to do that."

Looking down at my phone, I realized I needed to head to the chicken spot and then to shorty's house. The last thing I wanted her to think was that I had planned to stand her up. Wynner lay back down on the bed while Qua covered her up and kissed her on the forehead. He scooted in next to her, flicked the TV on, and got deeply involved in some criminal show.

"I'm 'bout to dip. . . . Jah, you need a ride home?"

Jah looked from me to Wynner, who was yawning and getting all comfy under Qua, and nodded his head. "Yeah. She 'bout to sleep, so I'll ride out with you."

"I'm 'bout to go see a shorty," I warned him ahead of time, and he was still with the shits.

Walking over to Wynner, I kissed her on the forehead and headed out of the room. She knew I would be up here later to kick it with her before heading home. I allowed Jah to do what he had to do and went to bring my whip around the front. My siblings were my heart, and anything they needed, they knew I had them. Until Wynner was in her own apartment, I was going to continue to sit up here with her, and I didn't give a damn that her husband was here.

It took me no time to find my car and pull around front. By the time I pulled around, Jah was coming out of the automatic doors. He was always front-seat riding with me, so I already knew the drill. He hated when people acted like he couldn't do shit for himself. With ease, he opened the door and slid right into the seat.

Taking his wheelchair, I folded it up and set it in the back. Then, I jumped back in the front seat, as he was putting his seat belt on, and I pulled away from the hospital. We were quiet for a minute as I drove through the streets, trying to remember where I saw a damn Popeyes at. When I realized I had to head to the hood, I hit a U-turn in the middle of the street and headed there.

"What's her name?" Jah broke our silence and my concentration on these damn bumpy-ass streets.

"Remi."

"What happened to Kandle? You know she gon' trip when she find out there's another chick taking up your time."

"It ain't even like that yet. Plus, she work with Kandle, so if she does end up taking up my time, they can handle that shit on their own."

"Kandle is a duck-ass ho," Jah's ass randomly blurted. I knew he couldn't stand her because she always had something smart to say when she saw him, but, damn.

"Damn, so I can't wife her?" I joked with him.

"Hell nah. Where we going?" He stared out the window, trying to piece together where we were headed.

"Popeyes."

"For what? You don't eat that shit."

"Shorty asked me to pick her some up. You want something while I'm in there?" I asked as I double-parked in front.

Jah had pulled his gun from his back, checked the clip, and set it in his lap. Ever since he was shot, he was always on point with the burna. "Nah, I'm straight."

Hopping out of the whip, I went inside as I Facetimed shorty. She picked up after a few rings with her hair all over her head. "I thought you had forgotten about me," she smiled.

"Nah, I would never do that. What you want, though?" She made a face and decided on what she wanted and told me. "That's all you want?"

"Yes, thank you."

"Bet. Send me your address now, or I'm gonna eat this shit myself."

Rolling her eyes, her screen went black, and then she came back on to the screen. "Sent. See you when you get here."

"Bet."

After I ordered her food, I hopped into the whip and headed toward her crib. Jah tucked his gun away, and we were chilling while driving across the Verrazano Bridge. "My nigga, I hope she's worth it with this expensive-ass toll. What the fuck they hiding in Staten Island, Jesus?"

"Shut up, nigga. She seem like she may be. I mean, what the fuck else I got to lose? I ain't got shit else to do, so I might as well kick it out here."

"While we out this way, make sure to run past the spots and see what the fuck is going on. These niggas won't expect to see you."

"Bet. You didn't even have to tell me. I already had that in my mind."

Her crib wasn't too far from the bridge, so I was calling her to come down ten minutes later. She lived in the projects, but the shit was near hella houses, so was it even considered the projects? It was hella white people walking their dogs and acting like this shit didn't say New York City Housing Authority out front.

"Damn, who that with her?" Jah damn near screamed out the window, as if I didn't have it rolled up. He was licking his lips and shit while unbuckling his seat belt.

"Shit, how the fuck would I know? She didn't tell me she was bringing somebody with her." Getting out of the whip, I came around the car and leaned on the hood.

Baby came down with a pair of tight-ass black biker shorts that showed all those hips, thighs, and ass. If I were her nigga, I would have been sending her ass upstairs coming down like that. Hell, I wasn't even her nigga and was still about to do the shit. Then, she finished the outfit with this tight-ass crop top and a pair of Vans. Shorty had put a brush to her hair, and it was pulled up in a huge bun on top of her head.

"Your man let you come down with those little-ass shorts on?"

"Yep, he told me to come get this chicken that I've been craving all day. How you doing?" She stepped in and gave me a huge hug. My hands found their way down to her ass and gripped both ass cheeks.

"Oh, word. Tell that nigga that I'm ready to give you more than this chicken."

She giggled as I whispered in her ear. "All I want is chicken, nasty." She hit me in the arm and then leaned off me. It was a good thing that she did because I was ready to fuck the shit outta her on the front of this car.

"Well, get the damn chicken because I want some." The girl with the blond haircut interrupted us.

"Uzi, this is my sister, Tweeti. . . . She was bored and decided to come down and chill with us too."

"She can come chill right here on my lap," Jah commented as he rolled the window down. My tints were so dark that you couldn't see inside my whip, and he scared Remi.

"Boy, I'll break your damn legs with all of this," Tweeti shot back. "Not to mention, you're probably one of those on the low chubby chasers."

Jah laughed as he rested his arm outside the window. "How about you come on and find out."

It was no secret that Jah liked thick women, and that's all you saw on his arm. Come to think of it, I never saw him with a skinny chick. They all had meat on their bones, which is how he liked them. Seeing that Remi's sister was a thick chick, I knew he wasn't going to leave without getting her number.

"You couldn't handle me even if you tried." She rolled her eyes.

Remi stood in front of me with a smirk on her face. "I can't believe you showed up. Every time I tell someone where I live, they act like I live in Georgia or something."

"Real niggas do real things." Walking around the car, I pulled out the bag with her chicken and handed it to her. "You gonna invite me upstairs?"

She and her sister both had this look on their face that told me that I didn't want to come up. "Uh, my mom is up there and acts crazy when we have company. Corny, I know, but I still live with her, so I have to respect her rules."

"We might have to change that real soon."

"Come sit on the steps with me." She motioned me with her head to follow her. I sat on the handrail as she got comfy on the stairs with her chicken. "I swear, this chicken taste like everything."

"You got grease all dripping down your lips and shit."

"Shut up. How's everything with you, though? Why you going through people to get my number?"

"'Cause when I like what I see, I gotta follow up on it."

"Oh, really? What about Kandle? She was all on you like you two have something going on."

"Me and Kandle is chilling."

"She know you're chilling? The problem I have with that is that she'll come to me about you and her chilling." She did fake air quotes with her free hand. "My job is how I pay my bills, and Kandle is known for getting girls fired if she doesn't like them. Joey keeps her around because she's one of the top strippers there."

"You don't have to worry about her. I'll handle her, and you'll have no worries."

"So, you and her *are* fucking around. She walked over to us like she was your girl, so it makes sense."

"She's not my bitch." I raised my voice. Kandle's ass was always doing shit like she did last night so people would believe she was my girl.

"Somebody getting mad," Remi teased.

"Nah, I just hate when shorty make it something that it's not. She got the whole club thinking I'm her nigga, so no other girls will dance on me. Shit is mad annoying to me."

"Well, maybe you need to stop fucking her and making her think otherwise," she suggested. "I mean, Kandle has been walking around talking about this new man, but I didn't know it was you. Y'all niggas kill me, though."

"How?"

"You probably be all laid up with that girl and wanna claim she's not your chick. Yet, you fucking her, probably taking her out and whispering sweet nothings in her ear when you fucking."

Remi had me figured out halfway, so I had to chuckle. When I was with Kandle, all I was thinking about was getting that box. So, yeah, I told her what she wanted to hear and took her a few places. Did that mean she was my girl? Hell nah, so why the fuck was this *my* fault in the first place?

"Here you go thinking you know my life and shit. What am I supposed to do? Hit and quit the shit?"

"Yep, especially if you don't have no desire to be in a relationship with li'l baby. Plus, she's always in the private room, so eeeh."

I already knew how Kandle got down, so when people called themselves trying to put me on to her, I was already two steps ahead of them. Kandle drove a BMW truck, had a condo, designer clothes, and always had money in her pockets. She didn't have to work at the strip club; yet, I think she did the shit just to piss me off. That was probably the biggest reason why I would never wife her. Why the fuck would I want a chick that was showing all my shit on the stage every night?

"Shorty, you ain't telling me shit that I don't already know. Why you working behind that bar half naked? You might as well be on the stage."

"Uh, not the hell I'm not. Wearing short shorts is one thing, but showing my ass and everything while fucking in the back is another. During the day, I work, and I work at the club at night for extra money."

"What you do?"

"Wipe ass," she bluntly stated.

"The fuck?"

"I work in the hospital as a patient care assistant, so all I do is wipe ass and take vital signs all day," she further explained.

"Shit, it's a job. You gotta do what you gotta do to feed your family."

"That's one thing you're right about. Look like your brother feeling Tweeti." She pointed to Tweeti pulling his wheelchair out of the back of my whip.

"Why you not surprised that he's disabled?"

"I'm around disabled, sick, and old people all day. He's fly as fuck, though," she commented on Jah's outfit.

"Your sister doesn't seem surprised either."

"Bro, you acting like we're shallow chicks who would feel some way about a man being in a wheelchair. We're from the hood and know how that goes. He got shot or some shit, right?"

Nodding my head, she smiled.

"You chill as fuck."

The one thing that I always worried about was how women would view my brother. I knew the nigga was dope as shit, and he did too. Yet, women tend to act funny as fuck with shit like that, so I always worried. Jah, on the other hand, was never worried about how a chick felt. He was always him and was quick to let a bitch know that he couldn't walk, but he could lay pipe down.

"I know." She bit into her chicken and crossed her legs. "You ready to tell me your real name?"

"Hell nah. Why you trying to get all deep into my business?"

"'Cause you all deep into mine."

"How you figure?"

"You in front of my building, so you know where I lay my head."

"Yeah, whatever. What you doing for the rest of the day? Come to the club with me," I told her.

"Why? I'm off from work, so I'm not interested in going back until I'm on the clock."

"Damn, I'm just trying to chill with you tonight. What you wanna do?"

She finished off her chicken and biscuit and then smiled. "I made some good tips last night, so I wouldn't mind you taking me to the mall to get some outfits."

"You really wanna go to the damn mall?"

"Uh, yeah. I don't have a car and been putting it off because I didn't feel like paying for a cab or taking the bus," she explained further.

"You gonna let me take you shopping?"

"No, I got paid real nice last night, so I can pay for my own things." She denied me my chance to blow some money on her.

"Bet. Let's find out if your sister and my bro gonna ride or what." She finished the soda that came with her food and stood up, wiping the crumbs she had accumulated on her little-ass shorts. "Nah, baby, you gonna have to change those damn shorts."

"Uzi, you're *not* my damn man, so you not about to dictate what the hell I wear." She rolled her eyes and walked down a few steps, then passed me. Although I was complaining about her shorts, my ass couldn't stop staring at how her ass shook with each step she took. Remi tossed the box of chicken in the trash and then walked back over to her sister.

"I'm gonna kick it with Tweeti for a second," Jah told me before I could fully make it over there.

"How you gonna get to the crib?"

"One of my shorties going to come scoop me. . . . I'm straight," he winked, reminding me that he had his gun on him.

"I don't know why he trying to stick around. I'm involved with someone, sooooo . . ." Tweeti rolled her eyes.

Jah had a smirk on his face as he rolled closer to her. "And, like I told you, I'm trying to take that nigga's place. Matter of fact, I don't even need to try. I'm *gonna* take his place."

Remi snickered as she leaned against the passenger side of my whip. "Tweet, you know damn well you don't have a man."

"You're right. I have *men*," she shot back.

"Your point is? The only person I fear is the man upstairs and my mama. You gonna let me take you out or nah?"

"Uzi, right?" she turned to me. "Take your damn brother home, please. I don't have time to be playing home health aide right now."

Jah laughed as he grabbed a handful of her ass, and she slapped his hand. "I need one, so why not?"

Jah knew damn well he didn't need a damn home health aide. Even when he had got shot, he never asked for one, and when my mother insisted on hiring one, he shut her down. He lived alone, dressed, and basically cared for himself. His crib only had rails in his bathroom. Other than that, everything was regular, and he adapted to doing shit on his own. Hearing him say he needed a home health aide was funny as fuck to me.

"You aggy as fuck. Where y'all going?"

"To the mall. I need to get some clothes and stuff," Remi explained.

"Y'all mind if I come along? I need to get me some winter shit too. . . . Oh, can I borrow some money?" she asked her sister, who rolled her eyes.

"You can have my money," Jah pulled her close to his chair, and she moved away from him. "Baby, why the fuck you keep moving from me?"

"Jah, if you don't quit touching me, nigga."

"Let me take you shopping."

"All I need is a sugar daddy that don't want no sugar. . . . You willing to be that?" she looked down at him, skeptical.

We all laughed because she was dead-ass serious with what she had said. "Look at it like this, I don't want no sugar right now."

"Sounds good enough to me. . . . Y'all gonna let me and my new best friend ride with y'all?" She rubbed the top of Jah's head.

"I don't mind. Uzi?" Remi put me on the spot. I wanted to tell them both that they couldn't ride, and I planned to take Remi out after the mall, but I nodded my head and told them to come on.

Remi thought she was slick, but I was going to get her to myself sooner than later, so she better brace herself. Just from kicking it for a quick minute, shorty had me all open. Her fine ass had me ready to let all these bitches go.

"Where you at, Mrs. McKnight?" I called as I walked through my parents' mansion.

This wasn't where we grew up, but where we moved once my pops started making bread. The hood was all we knew growing up. My mama was the most bourgeois chick on the block with her three kids. Bitches hated her because even though my pops didn't have the type of money he has now, he still made sure we had everything we needed. My mama didn't hang with chicks and didn't associate herself with chicks that wouldn't hesitate to take her spot. Instead, she focused on raising us, holding my father down, and being the wife that he married. When he finally moved us out of the hood, I was around 15 and was pissed. All my homies still lived in the hood, and here I was, moving to this big-ass crib in the middle of nowhere.

"I'm in the office, Parrish," she called back to me.

After walking down the long-ass hallway, I came to her office. My mother didn't work and never worked. My father had always taken care of her and instilled in us that you had to take care of a woman. A woman's place was to be at home with the kids, not punching someone's clock. I could respect it because this was something he promised my mother and lived up to the word. For me, if my chick wanted to work, that was cool. It was something she could do while I handled business and have that little bit of change to fill her tank or something.

"What you in here doing? Trying to act like you handle business?" I joked. Instead of working, my mother held down my father and his business. When I told her that she worked, she disagreed. She claimed she was merely helping her husband out with his businesses.

"I handle all the business under this roof . . . and some under yours too."

"Mine too? How you figure?"

"Who do you think stayed on your contractor's ass to finish the house? You would still be in that condo if it wasn't for me."

"You right."

"Anyway, to what do I owe this small visit? 'Cause I know you gonna run up outta here soon as you ask for something."

"Ask for something? Why would I ask for something, Mama?"

Pursing her lips, she side-eyed me. "Okay, so to what do I owe this small visit?"

"Dang, Mama, why it gotta be small?" She laughed and waved me off. "Nah, I just came over to see how you doing. Where's Pops?"

"He's out of town this week."

"Oh, okay. Ma, I fucked up."

"Lord, what did you do now, Parrish?" She stopped messing around on the computer and stared at me.

"I ended up messing around with Li—"

She held her hand up and cut me off. My mama knew about Lira and couldn't stand the ground she walked on. When we were younger, she always warned me about her, and it turned out she was right. You would think that after she warned me, I would have stayed away. What can I say? I was a sucker for a phat ass and pretty smile.

"Lira is a gold-digging slut, Parrish. How many times have we had this discussion? The reason you all went through what y'all went through was because of you. She never gave you a voice in the matter," she scolded. "You need to stop messing around with that child. All she wants is to be in your pockets."

"Ma, you wilding right now. I know how to handle myself when it comes to Lira."

"Oh, do you? Did you know how to handle yourself when shit went left?"

"Here you go, always bringing this up." I sucked my teeth and slouched lower into my chair. My mother never forgot shit and always liked to bring old shit up.

"It's still very much valid. You two both like to go on like it never happened; that's fine, but I'm not going to play pretend and act like I haven't lied to my husband to keep this secret of yours buried."

"Ma, I'm not getting into this with you. I came by to talk to you about it, but here you go scolding me like I'm a little-ass kid. I'm not Wynner, so you can save your speeches for her."

"As long as you are still walking around here calling me mama, I'm *always* gonna give you a speech and treat you like a child because you're my damn child." She hit her hand on the desk, shaking the glass figurines on it.

"Love you, but I gotta dip." I stared at my phone and acted like I had got called to handle business. She knew I was lying from the look on her face.

"Yeah, handle business. As always," she mumbled as I kissed her forehead and headed out of her office.

My mama was my queen, and I had the utmost respect for her. She always looked out and had been there when

Jahquel J.

I needed her the most. Still, that didn't mean I had to tell her everything anymore. She still acted like I was this 18-year-old boy that she raised, when, in fact, I was a grown-ass man handling business that I needed to. Mama was my world, but I kept her ass at an arm's distance to preserve the relationship we had.

Wynner

I wished I could blame this hospital stay on my lupus, except I couldn't. Uzi thought that I was here because of me getting sick again, but that was the furthest from the truth. Sometimes, I wished I could go into a hospital without my entire family rushing to come to visit me. Don't get me wrong. I appreciated my family and their concerns. I never wanted to sound ungrateful or like I didn't care that my family showed up and out for me. Yet, I would like to disappear for a week without my brothers sending someone to my house because they thought something was wrong with me. It pissed me off that they didn't trust that my husband would make sure that I was all right. Qua was my entire heart, and he would die before he let something happen to me. This time, my hospital stay was because I miscarried yet another one of our babies. For the life of me, I couldn't understand why this kept happening to me. All I wanted to do was to give my husband the baby he had been asking for. Qua was so understanding about the situation. He worried more about me than anything and kept me in good spirits.

The issue with fertility was a sore subject for me, so the only people that knew what I was going through were Jah, Qua, and myself. My mother always wanted to know what was going on with me, but I couldn't bear to tell her what was really going on. Uzi wouldn't understand because his relationship with Qua was just with work. He didn't hang with him outside of handling business and only visited our condo when I was there. Family was everything to me, and all I wanted was for my oldest brother and husband to get along. Jah didn't care for Qua when we first were married and stayed away. After his accident, he saw how Qua was at the hospital every day and making sure that he was fine. Their relationship started, and neither of them forced anything.

Jah would come over to check on me, and then he would spend some time kicking it with Qua. I prayed that he would tell Uzi that my husband wasn't that bad; yet, Uzi was so stubborn and didn't like to hear anything. One day, I prayed that they could get along for the sake of me. Eventually, God was going to bless me and make me able to carry a child into this world, and I wanted both my husband and brother to be able to get along. When they both were in the same room, you could feel the tension in the air, but nobody liked to speak on it.

"Baby, you good?" Qua gently nudged me when he came back into the room. He had left to walk Jah down and talk about business.

When it came to business, the men never discussed anything with me. They kept everything between the three of them. The only thing I knew about their business was that it made a lot of money and afforded me to live like a princess. While other women my age would have loved the position I was in, I couldn't stand it. All I wanted was to work a regular job and contribute to my bills like my husband did. When I brought the situation up to Qua, he forbade me to get a job. He claimed I was sick too often, and I didn't need to be stressing out while working a job that I didn't need.

"I'm fine. Did the doctors talk to you and tell you when I can come home? All they keep doing is ignoring me. Qua, I'm not a child, so stop telling them to keep things from me." I sat up in bed.

"Why you think I tell them that, Wyn? Each time they break something to you, you get in this mood and cut off everyone. Trust that I know what's good for you."

Rolling my eyes, I crossed my arms and stared out the window. "You say you can't stand the way Uzi treats me; yet, you do the same thing."

"Nah, your brother needs to step back and allow me to do what I need to do as a husband. I've always had your best interest at heart, and the nigga act like I haven't. Shit didn't go his way, which is why he can't forgive me. Everything is always good with your brother only when shit is going his way."

"I don't want to talk about this anymore. What are they saying?"

"They don't know why you keep miscarrying, babe. They thought for sure the bedrest would have helped the situation, but it didn't. I think we both need to take a break from the baby shit and clear our minds. . . . It's stressful as fuck."

My heart broke when Qua said those words to me. More than anything, all I wanted to do was bring a baby into this world. I couldn't work, and I did nothing all day, so you would think growing a baby inside of me and then delivering it would be the easiest thing. All I heard in the past few months was *sorry* and *you can try again.* Each time I surprised my husband with a heartfelt card or an announcement of my pregnancy . . . We were hit with the bad news that I miscarried.

"If that's what you think is best." I sniffled and lay back on the bed. Qua pulled the covers over me and kissed me on the forehead.

"I'm glad you're in agreement. I have to make a run to the crib. I'll be back in a few." He kissed me once more and left the room.

Sometimes, I felt like I wasn't good enough for Qua. He was older than I and could probably find another woman that could give him the one thing he wanted: a baby. I tried to be the best wife that I could, but I was always being sidetracked with being sick or being on bedrest because I couldn't carry a baby to term. It broke my heart each time the doctor told us bad news. The hurt was all over his face; yet, he tried to contain it so he could be the shoulder I needed to cry on. I worried about our marriage every day I opened my eyes, simply because I didn't want him to get tired of me.

"Hey, baby girl. How are you feeling?" My mama walked in with a McDonald's bag. It was only a matter of time before she found me.

"Mama, I told you that I'm fine, and you didn't need to come up."

Frowning, she ignored my statement and unpacked the bag with the food in it. "There's no way that my only daughter is in the hospital, and I'm going to stay the hell away. Wynner, you need to quit with this whole independence thing," she told me.

"Mama, I'm grown. You don't go checking on Jahquel and Parrish the way you do me."

She slapped a burger with fries down on my lap, then set the McFlurry on the bedside table next to me. "Jahquel and Parrish are my boys and will do what they do. You're my only girl, and as long as these feet are wearing Red Bottoms, I will be chasing you around in them." My mother stomped Louboutin pumps on the hospital floor.

At 49, my mother didn't look a day over 25. We were constantly asked if we were sisters whenever we went out together. Her body was still on point, and she worked out five times a week to make sure of it. She had Uzi at 16 years old when my father was still involved in the streets. Two years later, she had Jahquel, and then I came a couple of years after that. My father wanted a girl so badly that he wasn't going to stop until he got one. When I was born, the whole world stopped, and that's when my father decided to leave the game for good. It didn't mean he wasn't still getting to the money, because he was. The McKnight name ran long in the streets and in the corporate world. With my father investing money in oil, stores, and a bunch of other stuff, there was no way we would run out of money.

Although my father liked to play coy, I knew he still had a hand in what Uzi was doing. A zebra didn't change its stripes, so there was no way he was sitting back and not giving his two cents into what Uzi was doing. Everyone constantly compared Uzi to my father back in the day, so I knew my father had his hands in it somewhere.

"What are the doctors saying?" She sat in the seat beside the bed, crossed her legs, and sipped her coffee.

"The same thing they always say. I'm fine, really." Lying to my mother wasn't the easiest thing because she was always in my corner, so whenever I lied to her, I felt bad about it.

"Who you think you're fooling, Wynner Marie?"

Closing my eyes, I tried to yawn to act as if I were tired. "Mama, what are you talking about?"

"Wynner, if you don't want to tell me what's going on in your life, I have to respect that. You're a married woman, and what goes on inside your home is your business," she laid the guilt trip on thick for me.

Usually, when she got like this, I always broke down and told her what was wrong or going on. This time, I couldn't fathom telling my mother that I could get pregnant easily; my womb just wouldn't hold a child, however.

"Mama, there wouldn't be any other reason why I'm in here besides my lupus. I'm really tired of the boys being up here and disrupting my peace."

"You know your brothers mean well and love you, Wyn."

"I do. Parrish is just annoying with the way he goes about it. Why can't he be more like Jahquel?"

"They're two different men with two different personalities. Parrish needs more time to come around to Qua. He's not like the rest of us and can hold a grudge for the rest of his life."

"Mama, Daddy was pissed more than he was, and he has accepted Qua. Why is it so hard for Parrish to do the same? He acts like he's my father instead of my brother."

"He's your big brother, and he's always going to act like this. You're the baby of the family, and we all just want the best for you. When you married Qua, we didn't know if that was the best thing for you. Seeing how he loves and treats you like a queen, I know he's the best for you. It's just going to take your brother a little more time."

"It's been five years. Parrish needs to change his attitude about things, or I'm going to cut him off." My mother was shocked by my choice of words, but I was serious. Parrish thought he could say and do whatever he wanted and no one was supposed to feel any type of way. Qua didn't deserve for him to have slick comments every time he came around. Yes, he was hurt that we ran off and had gotten married, but he needed to see that I was happy, and it was the best decision of my life.

"Now, you're not about to cut your brother off for this. Parrish needs time like I just stated. Wynner, your brothers are everything to you, so I know you're lying about cutting Parrish off."

"When it comes to my husband, I'll do whatever I need to do. I'm married now, and I can't continue to allow Parrish to drive a wedge between my marriage with his hatred for Qua."

"He doesn't hate Qua."

"So, what else would you call it?"

"He dislikes him, and they will fix their issues. Don't push it and let it happen, Wyn."

Instead of going back and forth with my mother, I turned over and closed my eyes. It was draining trying to convince her that Parrish was being stubborn and a jerk. He was her oldest boy, and she would ride for him until the wheels fell off. In my mother's eyes, Parrish did no wrong.

"I see you're all in your feelings, so I'll get going. Eat that food because you need some food in your stomach." She kissed me on the cheek and left the room. At last, I was able to chill out and not be bothered with my family's nonsense. Closing my eyes, I nestled close to the pillow and fell asleep.

It had been three days since I was released from the hospital and back home. The doctor still wanted me to take it easy and get as much rest as I needed. After being in the hospital and being in bed all day, the last thing I wanted was to be laid up in bed at home. The first day I had gotten home, Qua made sure I stayed in the bed all day. For half the day, he lay in bed with me until he had to pack to go on a work trip. Parrish was sending him down to Miami to meet with one of the men he did business with. I hated that my husband had to be away from me for a couple of days, but I knew that Qua was doing all of this because of me. Sometimes I wished he didn't have to work so hard for the things that we had.

The buzzer sounded, distracting me from the cup of once-hot coffee sitting in front of me. Walking over to the wall camera, I saw Jah downstairs and buzzed him up. Jah was my favorite of both my brothers. He was levelheaded and understood things first before he blew up. Still, he was a menace and had a temper that would scare Jesus himself. Ever since he was shot, he had calmed down a lot and handled a lot of the behind-the-scene things that Parrish needed him to handle. When I heard the door chime, I held the door open, and he rolled into my condo.

"How you feeling?" he asked as he reached up and hugged me.

"I've had better days. What brings you over?"

Since Qua had left for Miami, I'd been in the house cleaning, watching TV, and just lying around. I didn't have friends because most females wanted to befriend me only because of who my brothers were. Besides my mama, I didn't have any women that I spoke with or could vent to.

"You been in this house since Qua went to Miami. He's going to be there for a few days extra to finalize some deals."

"Why couldn't he tell me that?"

"I'm sure he was, but I felt the need to tell you anyway. Let me get you out of the house tonight and take you out to dinner," he offered.

The offer sounded tempting; yet, I didn't want to get dressed and do anything. All I wanted to do was stay in the house to sulk about another baby that I miscarried. The blame I put on myself hurt so badly that I got chest pains from it. Why did I have to go through all the stuff that I did? It was like I was being punished for something that I didn't know I did.

"I appreciate it, Jahquel. I ju—"

"I'm not even trying to hear shit you 'bout to tell me. Wyn, I get you miscarried, and the shit probably hurt like hell, but you can't lock yourself in the crib each time it happens."

"Why can't I? It's a tough pill to swallow. Qua wants a baby, and that's the only thing that he has ever asked from me, and I can't give it to him."

"You acting like you don't have a husband that understands shit. He understands that you're doing all you can do to carry this baby. Right now, God has other plans for both of you, and you need to listen to that, Wyn. Now, go get dressed because I'm going to take you out to dinner, and we might go by the club."

"What club? Y'all never want me in the club."

"We go to the strip club. Tonight, I'm going to make an exception for you."

Smiling, I debated if I felt like declining his offer. When he gave me the stern eye, I turned on my heels and went into my closet to find something to wear. It wasn't every day that I went to a club with my brother. Although it was the middle of the week, I was excited to get out of the house and have a drink to take my mind off things.

Walking into my closet, I fingered through the wall of dresses hanging there. My closet was coordinated by colors, sizes, and seasons. It was nippy, so I settled on a plum-colored dress, black moto leather jacket, and a pair of black-studded biker boots. Heels would have complimented the outfit well, but I just didn't feel like slipping my feet into heels. Finishing off the outfit, I grabbed my black Future hat and Chanel purse.

It took me under an hour to shower, apply makeup, and get dressed. Qua always complained about how I took forever to get dressed. Seeing how quickly I was dressed, I knew he would have been impressed with my timing. When I came out of my bedroom, Jah was lying across my couch with his feet kicked up with the remote in his hand, watching the sports highlights. It amazed me how he did everything for himself without any help. My mother said it was a pride thing, and that his pride wouldn't allow him to depend on anybody except himself.

"How do I look?" I spun around in front of the TV.

"That damn dress too tight."

"Really, Jahquel? I'm *not* a little girl anymore, and I have hips, thighs, and curves to show off. Blame ya mama," I giggled as I checked to make sure I had everything inside of my purse I would need.

While I set the alarm and checked for my wallet, Jah pulled himself back into his chair, and we headed out. I loved spending time with my brothers when they weren't on my case about my life. It was crazy how they were always on my case about stuff when I was the youngest one, but now I was married, had my own place, and was more responsible than they were at times. Still, I knew it came from a good place, and they would always worry because I was their younger sister.

"We're painting the town red tonight, huh?" Jah laughed as we walked down to the parking garage where my car was.

For my birthday last year, Qua surprised me with an all-matte-pink Audi. He knew my favorite color was pink and how much I wanted a pink car. When he surprised me with the car, I tossed my panties, bra, and anything else I had on that night at him. Although it was my birthday, he was blessed with some bomb birthday sex for the whole night. Grabbing Jah's wheelchair, I struggled to put it in the backseat. He offered a few times to help like I was going to let him.

"Okay, where do you want to go for dinner? I could really eat a horse right this second." I cranked my car up and pulled out of the parking garage.

"Nobu is your favorite spot, so I guess we can head there."

"Yass, you know the way to my heart. I haven't been there in a few months. I wonder if the chef changed the menu." Jahquel laughed as I pondered to myself.

My entire family knew that was my favorite place to eat. I frequented that restaurant so much that the chef knew me by name and always sent special desserts to my table. Spending this time with Jah meant the world to me. He knew when Qua was away, I was always so lonely since I didn't have friends. It wasn't that I couldn't have friends; it was that I didn't trust anybody. All throughout high school, girls fawned over both Jahquel and Parrish. At one time, I had two friends that I called my besties. They would come over to our house, spend the night on the weekends, and we were always around one another. One year, my mother decided she was going to throw me a slumber party and invite them over.

What was supposed to be the happiest night of my life turned out to be one of the worst ones. In the middle of the night, I went to the bathroom and found one of them sucking Uzi off. Then, the other one fucked Jah and didn't say anything. The only reason I found out was that she couldn't keep quiet and spilled the beans to some girls around school. Imagine my surprise when all the girls in the twelfth grade wanted to come to my house for a sleepover! It was then that I decided that I didn't need friends if that was going to always happen. I wanted someone that was going to hang with me, not because my brothers could possibly come around or because they wanted to fuck them.

We arrived at Nobu, and the valet took the car and tried to help Jah out of the vehicle. "I said I know how to fucking get out of the car. Grab my damn seat out of the fucking back," he barked at the valet driver.

To know Jahquel was to love him. Since his incident, he was really angry and was quick to go off more than before. He wasn't sensitive when it came to him being paralyzed. It was when someone tried to help him. Jah could do everything himself, aside from a few things.

This poor valet driver just wanted to help . . . and got his head chewed off for it.

"I'm sorry," I apologized as Jah transferred himself from the front seat to his chair. When it came to walking, he would never be able to do that again. Still, he was able to stand on his legs for short periods of time.

"Fuck you apologizing for? He the nigga that thought he was about to toss my ass into my wheelchair like a rag doll," Jah continued to fuss as they held the door open for us.

We were seated right away since we were regulars. If I wasn't doing lunch here with my mother, then I was doing dinner with my brothers or Qua. I already knew what I wanted, so there was no need to look at the menu. Jah was focused on the menu with a scowl on his face. When shit happened to him, it was hard for him to get over it and move on.

"Please don't let that get you upset the whole entire night, Jahquel. He didn't know, so you didn't have to yell at him like that."

Jah shot his eyes at me one good time, and I quickly stared down at my menu. Then, I changed my mind and placed my menu back down. "I can go home if this is how you're going to act. You're not going to stare at me sternly like I'm your child. I have two parents, and their names aren't Jahquel Arlex McKnight."

He stared up from his menu again and smirked. "I swear you're a badass."

"I am when I need to be. You're letting one kind gesture ruin your entire night. Now, wave down the waiter so I can order those seared scallops that I love."

"Your ass about to turn into a scallop," he joked and waved down the waiter that was passing by.

After we placed our orders, we sipped on some wine and listened to the conversation around us. Jah turned his attention to me with a serious expression on his face. I knew he wanted to talk about the elephant in the room. It was something that I didn't care to talk about right now. What happened, happened, and there wasn't anything that I could do to take it back.

"Wyn, how are you really feeling? I know shit ain't sweet and all smiles, so be real with me." If there was one person besides Qua that I could keep it real with, it was Jah.

"How do you expect me to feel, Jahquel? I'm broken, feel like something is missing, and can't sleep. The only reason I'm out tonight is that you forced me out."

"I wish I could take the pain away from you, Wyn. I know how much you and Qua want a baby. It's going to happen, Wyn."

"Jah, I know you mean well, and I appreciate that, but I'm so sick of hearing that. I'm never going to be able to give my husband the baby he has been asking for."

He stared down at his drink in deep thought. "Is this baby about Qua, or do *you* actually want a baby?"

Qua told me when we got married that he wanted a baby. He also told me that he would wait a few years and allow us to enjoy our marriage. We've been to six different countries and been all over the U.S. enjoying life. Our finances were intact, we owned a condo, and didn't have any big issues in our marriage. So, when he told me last year that he was ready to start trying for a baby, I was ready too. The five years we've been married, Qua has worked his ass off to provide for us and never complained or asked for anything in return. I tried to work and do things, but with me always being sick, it was hard. Still, I was ready to get out there and work.

When it came to Qua and my family, they felt that I shouldn't work, so all I did was spend my days home waiting on Qua. The one thing he did ask for was a baby, and I felt that was one thing that I could give him. Imagine my surprise when I first found out I was pregnant. We were both over the moon and were planning names and the way we would raise him or her. Then, tragedy hit, and I miscarried. Tragedy continued to hit because each time I became pregnant, it ended with a miscarriage.

"I do want a baby. Why do you think I'm driving myself crazy trying to bring one into this world?"

"Because Qua has asked for one and you don't want to let him down. Wyn, you've never told me out of your own mouth you wanted to be a mother."

"Why do I have to tell you that? Maybe I told Qua that. Jah, where are you going with this conversation?"

"I'm just saying, stop being so hard on yourself about something you more than likely don't want."

He stared at me across the table and was reading my expression before he continued with what he had to say. "We're having a good time tonight. This isn't what I want to talk about."

Like that, he agreed and took a swig from his wineglass. Instead of talking about my life, Jah caught me up on his life. We continued to talk and eat our food while having a brother-and-sister night out. It was times like this that I lived for and loved doing.

Jahquel

"Yo, Remi!" I called over to Remi, who was down at the other end of the bar taking an order. Wynner had slid onto the bar stool next to me and was looking at the drink options. It seemed like she was just 19 years old trying to sneak into clubs, and now I was taking her out to the club to have a few drinks.

Unlike Uzi, I knew when to let Wynner be an adult. She would always be my baby sister, but I couldn't keep her sheltered and keep her from living her life. My sis had a husband that had her best interest at heart and would step in when he needed to. Once I realized that, our relationship had gotten better than it was in the first few years of her and Qua's marriage. The damage was done, so I could either sulk and be mad about the situation, or get to know the man that promised to protect and love my baby sister. When I got to know the real Qua, I realized that he was a man that was about his money. All he was concerned with was making sure my sister was taken care of.

"Hey, Jah, what you drinking tonight?" Remi came over, smiling as she popped the gum in her mouth. "Oh, you have a lady with you tonight," she observed.

"Nah, nothing like that. This my sis."

"Sis as in blood, or sis as in I'm fucking her, but we're gonna call each other sis and bro?" she questioned, and Wynner laughed.

"No, I'm his blood baby sister. None of that next shit you're chatting about," Wynner giggled.

"Oooooh, my bad. Hey, I'm Remi." She wiped her hand on her shorts and shook Wynner's hand. "Now looking at you, y'all do look alike."

"I'm Wynner. . . . What does a girl have to do to get some drinks around here?"

"Girl, tonight has been so damn busy. I just have to get those three men a drink, and I can come sit with y'all in a booth and bring a bottle."

"Shit, make it three bottles," I told her and slid my card across the bar top.

"I got you," she promised.

Everybody moved the fuck out of my way as Wynner and I rolled through the club. Sleazy-ass Joey was right behind us when he saw me walk in. "Jah, how you doing, man?" He held his hand out, and I just stared at it.

Joey was a typical manager at a strip club. If it didn't make dollars to him, it didn't make sense. I could relate to that; yet, what I couldn't relate to was how he recruited these young-ass girls. A few times, I had to go upside his head about having young-ass girls in the club. The last thing I wanted to worry about when going to see strippers was if a chick was young enough to be my little sister.

"I'm straight."

"Hey, Joey," Wynner hugged him.

"Wow, Wyn. You look amazing. How are you doing?"

"I'm doing well. Just enjoying a night out with big bro. The club looks amazing. I like the renovations."

"Yeah, the owners have been on my ass about making sure this place stays in good shape. Here's a booth, I'll have someone bring some drinks over and have a good night on me." He winked at Wynner.

Grabbing his knee with all my might, he winced in pain. "Stop eye fucking her, 'cause you not getting nowhere near her, a'ight?"

"Nah nah nah, it wasn't like that. Wyn is family," he tried to convince himself more than he did me.

If Wynner gave his ass a chance, he would be all on her like white on rice. So, all that shit he was trying to convince me of was bullshit. "Keep your fucking eyes forward when speaking to her, hear me?"

"You got it, Jah. . . ." His voice trailed off as he ran away soon as I let his knee go.

Wynner slid into the booth and laughed. "You caught that too, huh?"

"Yeah. Nigga so fucking thirsty, he already know I don't play about you, so I don't even know why he tried."

"A lot of people think because you're in a wheelchair you can't do much like you used to. Since what happened, you been real quiet and low-key, so you know how niggas get when someone gets quiet."

"Might be time to shake some people up."

"Maybe. But for tonight, let's have a good time, and keep Joey's creepy ass away from me," she made sure to add.

"You already know."

"So, who's ol' girl? I've never seen her when I come here."

"Oh, really? When the fuck you come here?" I liked to think that my sister sat at home and didn't get out much. Who the fuck was I fooling with that logic?

"Never mind all of that, who's the girl?"

"One of the shorties that Uzi is talking to."

"What happened to Lira?" If I were a chick, I would have rolled my eyes when she asked that question.

Lira was Kandle's real name. That bitch was like a thorn in my side. For the life of me, I didn't understand why Uzi chose to fuck with her sneaky ass. The bitch was a thirst box and was always about the money since we were younger. When Uzi started fucking with her back in the day, I told him that he needed to leave her ass alone. Still, he continued to fuck with her until he found out she was stripping. They stopped fucking around for a bit but always kept in touch. My mother hated the ground that Kandle walked on. It was one thing that I couldn't stand the bitch, but another when my mother didn't like her and had every reason why she didn't like her.

"He still fucking around with her. Her nasty ass should be shaking that fake-ass booty out here soon."

"Dang, you really can't stand that girl," Wynner giggled. "She's an airhead, but she's not all that bad like you're making her out to be."

"You only like her because she compliments you and always asking you where you get your stuff."

Laughing, she shook her head. "Well, I like someone to gas me up once in a while."

"Yeah, getting gas from that bitch might cause your ass to end up looking like Wendy Williams on that damn beach."

Wynner fell back onto the chair and kicked her feet while laughing. "Jahquel, you need to quit it. She's not that bad, and if Uzi likes her, then I love her."

"Nah, he's about to be all into Remi. . . . Wanna bet some bread?"

"You always trying to take my little bit of change. He and Lira have some kind of magnetic relationship; they always find themselves back to each other."

"Shit about to change with Remi. There's something about shorty that got Uzi's head open."

"Well, her body is the bomb, and she's pretty, so I wonder what else could have his mind open," Wynner's smart-ass shot back. "I'm not saying I'm Team Lira, because I'm not. I just know when to support Parrish with his girls."

"Wyn, you showing fake supporting ain't gonna make him accept Qua," I called her ass out. She knew she disliked Lira too, but she wanted to front like they were the best of friends.

"Man, whatever. Lira's here too tonight. I just saw her head to the back to change."

"You thought shorty wasn't about to get this bread? She 'bout to shake her stank shit all around this club and then try to fuck Uzi later."

"Thanks for the visual, Jahquel. Look, here comes Remi." She pointed and slid over so Remi could sit.

Remi placed the bucket with the bottles on the table, then set the glasses down beside them. She slid next to Wyn and touched her hair. "Your hair is so pretty," she smiled.

"Thank you. . . . I love yours too. Nice and curly," Wynner complimented her back.

"Shit, none of y'all gonna compliment me? I'm looking dapper and shit."

"Uh-huh. You probably came to ask me where Tweeti is," Remi called my bluff, knowing damn well that's why I came.

Shit, there was something about Tweeti's thick ass that made me want to know her more. Shorty had this short blond cut that just did something for me. Tweeti was just different, and the shit turned me on. The way she spoke her mind made my dick hard because I couldn't stand a chick that was all shy and reserved. Her light brown skin was the color of coffee after you dropped a little milk in it. Then, her eyes were this light green color. A nigga didn't know they were her real eyes, or if she had some contacts in that day. When you got to her nose, it was small and right in the center of her face with a piercing through it. Her body was just thick in all the right places for me. When it came to me, I loved my women thicker with more cushion for the pushing.

"Where she at, though?"

"You see him? All cheesing and shit." Remi poked fun when all I needed to know was the answer to my question.

"If you must know, she's going on a date tonight," Remi revealed. From the way she rolled her eyes, I could tell whoever the nigga was, she wasn't a fan.

"Oh yeah? Where they going?"

"Damn, Jah, why you all in her business like that?"

"Sylvia's. Tweeti never been and wanted to go."

"Call her right now and ask her where she's at," I told her, and she did as I said. Wynner stared at me with a smirk on her little face as she poured herself another cup of Cîroc.

Remi was on the phone with Tweeti and then stood up and left the booth. "I hope she's all right," Wynner said.

I held my hand up and rolled behind Remi as she walked outside of the club. She was saying something to Tweeti, but I couldn't make out the words. As I got closer, she spun around and jumped because she didn't expect to see me.

"Jah, you can't be rolling up on people like that." She tried to make light of the heated conversation she just had moments before.

"What happened?"

"He stood her up." Remi sucked her teeth. "I told her she needs to stop putting her all into these niggas and treat them how they treat her."

"How they treat her?"

"Tweet has so much confidence; yet, she lets these niggas who don't deserve her just do whatever they want. Like, dude was supposed to come and take her out. She's home and dressed, and he calls her to say he gotta make a run and can't make it. Then, she goes on Instagram and sees that he's chilling with some chick and his bros. The shit is unfair, man."

Staring up into her face, I could tell she was hurt for her sister. "I'm 'bout to catch a cab to y'all's crib. . . . Text me the address," I told her as I pulled up the Uber app on my phone.

"Don't worry about it, Jah. She'll go to bed. She doesn't seem like she cares anyway. I just know Tweeti, so I know the difference."

"Send me that information like I said. . . . Do me a favor too."

With her head down in her phone, she replied. "What's up?"

"I'm leaving Wynner with you. . . . Make sure she gets home and don't nobody fuck with her. She's a good girl and deserves to have a nice night out."

The cab pulled up, and I transferred myself to the back while he put my wheelchair in the backseat. See, this nigga knew that I wasn't about to play with his ass. Since I've been paralyzed, niggas thought I was a rag doll or something, like I didn't know how to do shit, and it pissed me off. Yeah, I could handle the situation different each time; yet, I only knew one way I could handle it. My mind was on Tweeti as we pulled away from the curb. Shorty was too dope to be stood up and not treated like a queen. Niggas these days didn't realize when they had a winner on their arm. Instead, they liked to hurt feelings and then go off with the next chick like it was nothing.

Chicks these days weren't good for shit except sucking my dick, and when I wanted some pussy, providing that. When it came to Tweeti, sex didn't even come across my mind. The shit wasn't even a thought, and all I wanted to do was chill with her. When we went to the mall, shorty balled out with my money, and I didn't have a problem with it. Shit, she told me ahead of time what it was, and I accepted that shit. The only reason I accepted it was because I knew she was going to be mine, eventually. She was spitting all that friend shit, but I knew she was going to be my girl. It was only a matter of time before she was my woman and niggas knew she was off-limits.

I don't know how to explain the shit, but when I saw her walking down those stairs in front of her building, I had a feeling I hadn't had in a long time. Like, I could get out of the whip and walk over to her. Since shit went down with me, I hadn't felt like that in a long-ass time. The streets weren't something you stayed in forever, and I knew that coming into it. Niggas wanted to see you doing better—yet, not better than them. When Uzi started taking over territory, they couldn't stand that we were bringing in more bread than they were, and they had to get their shit from us. Long story short, I was a target because of my older brother's success in the drug game. One night, I was staggering out of the club, fucked up from a night of drinking. We were turning up and getting bent as fuck because we had just secured this trucking distribution deal. Yeah, I should have been watching my back, and I shouldn't have been drunk as fuck.

There was a bunch of shit I blamed myself for when the doctors told me I may never walk again. One thing I did know . . . It was niggas from the Bronx that came and shot me. If there was one thing I was grateful for, it was to still be breathing this polluted-ass air. Uzi painted the town red when I was shot. We still don't know who was responsible to this day, but we know them niggas were from the Bronx, and they're no longer breathing. From being so athletic to being in a chair the majority of the day took some time. Hell yeah, I was bitter and cut my family off for the first few months. I constantly hopped out of bed thinking I could walk—and was met by the cold floor and the even colder reality that my legs didn't work the way they used to.

When it came to women, I wasn't stupid or naïve. I knew half of them only fucked with me because of my name and how much money I had. I'd be a fool to think these women wanted me for me. Since Uzi wasn't having them, they figured it would be easy to get in with the crippled brother. I allowed them to think that and went with the flow. After I got pussy, they were shown the door, and I never called them again. Shit, since they wanted to use me, I was about to use them first. They never even made it on a second date because I couldn't trust their asses. With Tweeti, I could tell she was different. Shorty didn't even blink when I asked her to take my wheelchair out of the back.

I dialed her number and waited for her to answer. When she clicked the phone, I dialed the number back the second time; this time, she answered. "Hello?"

"Yo, come downstairs."

"Jah? What are you talking about?"

"Just come downstairs and don't keep me waiting," I told her and ended the call.

Ten minutes later, we were pulling in front of her building. She walked slowly to the car and told the cabdriver she would get my wheelchair. Opening the door, she lined it up with the cab, and I was able to slip myself right into the chair. Today, she had on a long blond wig, and the shit looked fire on her. Her face was fully made up with makeup, and she was wearing a pair of gym shorts, a tank top, and slippers.

"Why do you take cabs and have people drive you places? You can move your legs, so I'm sure you can drive," she pointed out.

"I don't feel like it. Why drive when I can have people chauffeur me around all day, right?" I was fine to drive and had three cars I could pick from. They were all parked at my parents' crib because I didn't want to drive anymore.

"Whatever." She sighed and helped me onto the curb. "What are you doing here? Did Remi send you?"

"Nah, she told me about your little fuck boy that stood you up, so I'm stepping up."

"First off, you not stepping up no damn where . . ." Her voice trailed off as she laughed. I could take a joke and didn't get offended when someone cracked jokes, so when she said it, I laughed with her.

"Oh shit, you got jokes."

"I'm kidding, but, yeah, he stood me up, and I'm fine. It's part of life, and I'm not going to die because he didn't stick to his word."

"You gonna still give him a chance after this?"

"Probably. He's cool, and we're not together, so he doesn't owe me anything. I'm fine, Jah. I promise," she tried to convince me.

From the one time that I had met her, she was loud and outgoing. Tonight, she was being all quiet and shit and acting like she was shy. "I'm hungry as fuck, so come with me to get some food."

"I literally just changed out of my clothes. Do I really have to?"

"Yeah, my stomach rumbling like I haven't ate shit all day, even though I just had dinner with my sister like an hour ago," I revealed.

"You can come up to my room and order some food. I really don't want to go out tonight, so please don't make me."

"As if I could make you do anything."

Tweeti chuckled, and we headed upstairs. The house was quiet, with the exception of snoring coming from the living room. "Yo, who the fuck snoring like they worked twelve jobs today?"

"Evelyn . . . Ignore her. She'll find her way to her bedroom eventually," she replied nonchalantly. "Go down the hall. The second room on the right is mine." I watched as she went into the kitchen.

Thankfully, her hallway wasn't as narrow as I was praying it wouldn't be. There were cute baby pictures of both Remi and her. I noticed there weren't pictures of her moms anywhere, just of them two. When I turned the knob and opened the door, there was a queen-size bed with a purple satin bed set on it. Shorty had clothes hanging everywhere and boxes of shoes piled to the ceiling.

"I love fashion, so don't judge me." She came behind me and closed the door. "You want the air on? It's not all that hot, but Remi always complains that my room is always hot."

Taking off my sweater, I laid it on the bed and put the brake on my chair. Tweeti watched as I transferred myself over to her bed and got comfortable. "Nah, I'm straight. You could help a nigga take his shoes off, though."

"First of all, who told you to get your crippled ass on my bed?"

"Ain't gonna be too many cripples, blondie."

"Why don't you get offended? Each time I say something about you, you just roll it off your back. If it really bothers you, I won't do it anymore."

"Somebody getting soft," I joshed. "Nah, you gotta have thick skin dealing with some shit like this. Plus, Uzi always got the jokes, so I learned to adapt."

She leaned on the door and nodded her head. "How did this happen to you?"

"What the fuck is this? Twenty-one Questions? Let me ask you a question," I switched subjects. The last thing I wanted to talk about was how this shit happened.

"What's that?"

"Why you way over there instead of on your bed next to me?"

"Because I'm thinking about what I want to order to eat. Was that really your question?" She smirked and folded her arms.

Damn, there was something about the figure of a thick woman that I could appreciate. Every roll, curve, and lump had a story to tell. Tweeti's body definitely had a story that I wanted to know about. Niggas that complained about bigger women were pussies. I mean, you were allowed to like what you liked, but the moment when you started putting down a woman about her body was when you became a dub to me. I loved all types of women, yet my preference was a thicker woman. There was something about holding all those thighs and ass in my hands. Shit, I liked what the fuck I liked, and I dared a nigga to come at me about it.

"Nah, I wanna know where you and homie that stood you up stand."

Tweeti looked at me, and I could tell she didn't know how to answer the question. Each time she opened her mouth to speak, she closed it back. "We're good, I guess. He's not my man, and I'm not his girl, so it doesn't really matter where we stand, right?"

"It don't matter where y'all stand, huh?" I repeated her answer and chuckled.

"Don't even look at me like that, Jah. You want me to cut him off because he stood me up? I mean, I should, but I'll let him sweat next time he wanna chill."

"Make him sweat," I chuckled again.

"Stop repeating everything that I'm saying." She started to get irritated. "Why are we talking about my love life anyway?"

"Oh, you love this nigga?"

"Jah, if you don't cut it out." She laughed. "I don't love him, and we're chilling. He stood me up, so I got his card the next time he come around. Trust, I'm far from stupid, and things I do all have a reason behind them."

"What's the reason?"

"Um, he about to lace me with some bread. Why the hell you think I'm being nice about the situation?"

"For money? Dead ass?"

"Yeah. Unlike you, I don't have money coming out of the ass. He knows he fucked up, and he's gonna try to toss money my way to make me forgive him. That money will pay the bills I have and put money in my pockets."

"Man, that shit sound stupid. Get your ass a damn job like your sister. You see her out here fucking around with niggas for money?"

"You don't know my fucking life. Stop sitting here acting like you know me and my life. I'm not my sister, and how I decide to get money isn't your or anybody else's business," she snapped and walked out of the room.

If I could walk, I would have bounced. It took so much for me to get all the way upstairs, and then I transferred myself to her bed, so a nigga wasn't going anywhere. She was about to feel real awkward in her own spot. Tweeti was gone for a good thirty minutes, then walked back into her room like nothing happened. When she looked over at me on her bed, she sucked her teeth.

"I heard the front door close and assumed you left. What the hell you still doing here?"

"You trying to be funny?"

"No, why are you still here? Matter of fact, I don't know why you even showed up after Remi's big mouth told my business. I'm not interested in being more than friends with you."

Usually, that shit would stink a nigga's ego, yet I felt like she was lying. If she truly didn't want shit to do with me, she would have spazzed when she walked into this room and I was still sitting here.

"Shut the fuck up, Tweeti, and order some food. You leave me in here for thirty minutes, your room all cold and shit. I'm fucking hungry." I kicked my shoes off and took my socks off.

For some weird-ass reason, I couldn't stand being in the crib with socks on. It was something I did as a child and didn't think I would ever stop. Tweeti looked at me with a smirk on her lips and left the room. While she was gone, I pulled myself up toward the head of her bed and grabbed the remote from the bed table. Looking over to my left, she had a throw blanket, so I grabbed that shit and tossed it over my damn legs. Fuck is she? A damn vampire with all this cold going on in her room?

"I ordered some Chinese food." She took her shirt off and opened her closet. My tongue ran over my lips, and my dick got hard as she pulled a baggy white T-shirt on.

"How the fuck you knew what I wanted?"

"First off, Jah, you gonna watch who you coming at before I push your ass onto the floor." She pointed her finger at me. "Second of all, I ordered a bunch of food to pick from, so I need your money."

"Oh, I'm paying for all this shit you ordered, huh?" I dug into my pants pocket and peeled off a hundred-dollar bill.

"So, should I tip him or nah?"

"Yeah, like five dollars and bring me my damn change."

"I'm keeping it."

"If you keeping it, then I better be getting some head."

Her mouth dropped, and she stared at me and tried to figure out if I was serious or not.

"You serious?"

"Dead serious."

"I'll kick your little crippled ass." She walked toward me and punched me in the arm. "I don't fuck for money. You got me twisted with what you think I do to get money."

"Chill. I don't have to pay to get head. I'm fucking with you."

She sat beside me on the bed and got under her blankets. "Why are you here? We met one time, and you're in my house and bed."

"If memory serves me, you invited my ass up here. I just came to chill with you downstairs."

"You think you cute, huh?"

"Shit, that's what the shorties are telling me."

"Ugh, you're so cocky." She giggled and checked her phone. Her phone lit up in her hand, and she clicked *ignore*.

"You can answer. I'm not gonna fuck up your money."

She sighed and placed her phone on the night table beside her. "I'm not worried about you saying anything." She grabbed the remote and flipped through the channels. She decided on some HGTV house show.

"Why nobody locked you down?"

"Locked me down?"

"Yeah, why that pussy ain't on lock? You walking around here looking like a full-ass meal, and I wanna take a bite."

"Because niggas don't want to settle down. Or some of them like big girls and like to keep it on the low. I can't stand a down low chubby chaser."

"I like 'em chubby, so no need to hide or front like I don't."

"Hmm, we'll see about that. Let me see a chick on your arm that's thick."

"You don't need to see. . . . You 'bout to *be* that chick."

When the words left my mouth, she blushed. "Stop saying all the right things. I'm not going to sleep with you." She climbed out of the bed when she heard someone banging on the front door.

"I'm not saying the right things. I'm saying all the things that are true. I may be a lot of things, but I'm not a liar."

"Being that all the niggas I've dealt with turned out to be liars, I'm leery," she explained as she walked out of the room.

I didn't know what niggas she dealt with, but I wasn't one of them. At this point in my life, I didn't have time to play games with females. All the little cat-and-mouse games females liked to play, I didn't have time for. When I was interested in a chick, I put all my attention into her. There was no need for me to lie about my intentions when I was the one pursuing them.

"This nigga wasn't even satisfied with the five-dollar tip I handed him." She came back into the room with two bags, plates, silverware, and a bottle of soda.

"Greedy asses. They put duck sauce in there because they act like they can't give enough for the food. One damn duck sauce," I vented more to myself.

"Dang, you really mad about this duck sauce. They put a few in there." She checked the bag and put the food on the bed.

Her bedroom door opened, and a woman that she resembled stumbled in. "You ordered food and didn't think to ask if I wanted some," she slurred as she held on to the door.

Tweeti's face looked like she was defeated. Placing the plastic container down, she turned toward who I assumed was her mother. "Evelyn, go on and leave me alone. Go to your bedroom, and I told you about just walking into my room," she responded.

"Who the hell is this? Now, you're bringing niggas to the house?" the woman continued, not missing a beat.

"Get the fuck out of my room, Evelyn!" Tweeti screamed and pushed the woman out the doorway, then slammed the door.

At first, I was going to say shit. Then I thought about it, and that wasn't how I rolled. "Your moms?"

"Unfortunately," she plated the food. "You like Crab Rangoon?" she asked as she put food on to what I assumed was my plate.

"Never had it."

"First time for everything."

"She good?"

Tweeti stopped plating the food and stared at me. "What? I don't want to talk about it."

"You shouldn't talk to her like that. That's your moms, and you only get one."

"How about you live with her when she's high and falls asleep and has her head in the fridge? Or when she comes into my room in the middle of the night and talks in circles. I want you to try to live with her growing up and always high as hell, or lying about pain to get prescription pills. Until you live with that, don't tell me how to treat her."

"Shit, I thought she was drunk."

"No, she has a problem with pills. Has had a problem since I was young."

Shaking my head, what could I say? Shorty and her mother had a bad relationship, and my little words of wisdom weren't going to help her out, so I decided to drop the subject. "Bring my damn plate over here."

Laughing, she handed me a plate, poured me some soda, and then slid onto the bed next to me. We ended up watching some chick flick and laughing.

"I swear, this movie is hilarious," she giggled.

After we finished two plates of Chinese food, I got comfortable under her blankets. Tweeti was getting sleepy because her damn head kept nodding. She finally fell asleep on my arm and was snoring loud as fuck. Turning the TV off, I pulled the covers up farther on her and got comfortable.

I sent Wynner a quick text message before I fell asleep. *You home?*

Yes. Night, Jahquel.

Once she hit me back, I turned my phone off and set it on the nightstand, then lay down until sleep eventually found me.

Remi

When I walked back inside, Wynner was placing her phone back into her purse. She was so pretty, and I could see a few guys eyeing her from across the room. If I hadn't walked back in, the table would have been swarmed with different niggas trying to shoot their shot. Sliding back into the booth, she fixed her hair out of her face and stared at me with a smile on her face.

"Where's my hardheaded brother?"

"Umm, how do I tell you that he's getting into a cab to run to my sister?"

"Just like that," she giggled. "I might as well head on home. Jahquel promised me this whole fun night and then gonna bail on me. She better be worth it." She finished off her drink and grabbed her purse.

"You don't have to go home just yet. I'm off work and have nothing to do." I gently placed my hand on her forearm.

Placing her purse down, she smiled. "You don't have to hang with me. I know Jah probably told you to watch me or protect me, but that's not necessary. I'm gonna go straight home," she explained to me.

From the way she acted, I could tell she wasn't used to having friends. Looking at her hand, she had a huge wedding band on her finger, which told me she was spoken for. Wynner carried herself a different way than other females. She could have been in this club acting a fool. Yet, she was reserved and took a few sips from her glass every few minutes.

"Girl, I don't care what your brother told me. If I didn't want to hang, I wouldn't be trying to hang. You seem really cool, and I wanna pick your brain about your brother."

"Parrish?" she questioned.

Laughing, I shook my head at Uzi's real name. That's probably why he didn't want to tell me his name. "Wow, I've been trying hard to get his real name, and he wasn't trying to tell me."

Wynner giggled and picked her purse up. "These men are too thirsty, like they don't see that I'm married. If you don't mind, we can go to my condo and hang out," she offered.

"Shit, I'm down. Let me order an Uber. My treat."

"We drove; don't worry about it. Come on." She stood up, tossed a fifty-dollar tip on the table, and headed out. Before following behind her, I grabbed the money and shoved it into my pocket. Hell, I was the one who brought the bucket of bottles in the first place.

"I know it's annoying being the baby sister, right?" I asked as we walked down the block. The one thing I hated about the club was the lack of parking. If you got here early, you could get a good parking spot, but if you showed up later in the night, you would be parking a few blocks down . . . *if* you were lucky.

"It's so annoying because they never know when to stop. Jah has gotten so much better, but Parrish? He's a whole mess and thinks I'm still that little girl," she started venting. I could tell this pissed her off because she was gripping her car keys tightly.

"They care about you. I'm the same way about my little sister. She hates it, but then she realizes that she's all I have."

"I know it's love, but sometimes it's too much, and I get annoyed."

We arrived at her car, and it was then that I realized that she was just a princess complaining. Who the hell cared if my brothers were on my case if I was riding like this? It wasn't easy to ignore her designer clothes, but that was normal when it came to women being at the club. It's another thing when she is standing in front of a matte pink Audi like it's a regular-ass car.

"If your brother got you riding like this, I don't think you should be complaining," I halfheartedly joked.

Popping the locks, we slid inside. The pink leather seats matched the outside. This was a custom car, and they paid money to get it this way. "My husband bought it for my birthday. Parrish just buys me jewelry because he knows I love it."

I watched as she buckled her seat belt, checked her messages, and then pulled off. The way she moved was different than other females. "How old are you?"

"Twenty-five," she replied, making a left down the next block. "You?"

"Same age," I replied. "You're just so put together. Like, I wouldn't have expected you to be 25, even though you do look that age."

"Girl, I got married when I was 20 years old. My husband is 31, so I had to grow up pretty quick."

"Why did you get married so young?"

"I love him. Couldn't see myself without him, and he asked me if I wanted to marry him. It was one of the best decisions I've ever made in my life." Just by staring at her as she drove and spoke about her husband, I could tell the love was there.

Love was so beautiful to me when it was done right. Unfortunately, I had never been able to witness real love like some women did. Every time I got involved with a man, he always did some shit that made me question the whole relationship. With Shaq, he liked to

claim me as his girlfriend, yet didn't do shit that a nigga would do for his girl. I liked to be chased. It showed
me that the man was worth me slowing down and getting to know. Shaq was just fucking to me because he
came with a bunch of baggage. Between his three kids,
trash weed, and not being persistent, I only dealt with
him when I was bored. Part of the problem was me too.
I allowed him to call me when he wanted and still went
to hang with him. When did I stop carrying myself with
more pride?

"Since your brothers are overly protective, I'm guessing
they weren't happy that you married him, huh?"

"Nope. Jah has come around, but Uzi and my husband
don't get along at all."

"How old is Uzi?"

"Thirty-two."

I cleared my throat because I expected him to be older,
yet I didn't think he was in his thirties. He was a whole
grown-ass man and was interested in my young ass.
"Your brothers love you. Right now, it doesn't seem fair,
but when time goes on, you'll understand that it's all out
of love."

It wasn't too long before we were pulling up to a
building. She drove into the parking garage and pulled
into a spot that I assumed was for her apartment number.
Killing her engine, she grabbed her purse and got out.

"I'm happy to have someone come home with me. I hate
walking through here alone." She pressed the elevator
button, and we waited until it came from the third floor.
The parking garage was nice, so I didn't expect anything
less when it came to the inside of the building.

"Girl, don't mention it. I didn't have anything to do, so
coming to hang with you sounded fun."

"I don't have friends," she blurted like it was a disclaim-
er or something.

Laughing, we stepped into the elevator. "I could tell."

"Really? Is it that noticeable?"

"Uh, yeah. No girl is about to go to the strip club with her big brother. Especially since he's the protective type. It's all right because you're not missing anything by not having friends. Bitches are still messy, will want your life, and be jealous as fuck."

The elevator took us to the twentieth floor.

"In high school, I was the girl with the fine brothers to the girls. To the boys, I was the girl who they knew they better not try to step to. So, I never knew if people really wanted to be friends because of me, or because of who my brothers were."

"You did the right thing by sticking to yourself. Shit, I got a few bitches I need to clear out of my life because they're messy and about drama. Trust, you're not missing a damn thing. I actually like you, so I don't mind hanging out and doing stuff together. You would love Tweeti too."

Wynner was different; yet, she was cool, quiet, and wasn't all loud and flashy. She had nice things, but she didn't toss them in my face or hype them up like some people did. To her, these were regular things. To me, this shit was the bomb, and I would walk around with a fur coat all day long, telling bitches that I was better than they were. That was just me.

Wynner let us into her apartment, and it was gorgeous. Everything was either gold or beige, and the whole décor reminded me of something in the south of France.

"Your condo is beautiful," I complimented as she kicked her boots off, tossed her purse onto the couch, and went into the kitchen.

"Thanks. Want something to eat? I have some pizza bites and stuff. When Qua is away, I never really cook."

"I'm good with something to drink." Taking a seat on the couch, I saw so many pictures of her and her husband. Some of them were in other countries, and then some of them were regular selfies that had a fancy frame.

"Here you go." She handed me a drink and plopped onto the opposite couch. "I'm all about pictures, as you can see. Qua hates pictures, but he takes them for me."

"Aw, he seems like a great man. Why doesn't Uzi like him?"

"We ran off and got married, and he hasn't forgiven him for it. The funny thing is that our parents have gotten over it and accepted Qua."

"Damn. Tell me about him. I just feel like he's too good to be true, and we've only hung out once, but he was a gentleman. He wouldn't let me get out of the car without opening it first for me."

"Our father. My mother never lifted a finger when he was around. I was raised to have a man take care of me, and he was raised to take care of his woman."

Hearing that they were raised by both parents surprised me. That was almost rare nowadays. I was raised by both my parents, but they weren't together. So, when my mother told me I couldn't do something, I would go ask my father. They were never on the same page when it came to raising Tweeti and me.

"That's rare."

"Uh-huh." She raised her wineglass to her mouth. "On the outside, my parents are considered upstanding, but we all know my father cheated on my mother, and we have a little brother. My mother likes to act like we don't know my father was out there being a dog when we were younger. Now, he has his stuff together and treats her like a queen, but she had to go through hell and high water to get him to act right." I wasn't sure why she was revealing all of this to me during the first time we met.

"Have you met your brother?"

"Girl, I never looked into it. All I know is that my mother and father were screaming and yelling about some chick pregnant with his baby. Never looked into it or asked questions because I didn't want to know. All I acknowledge as my brothers are the two you met."

"Damn."

"Back to Parrish. He's sweet, hardheaded, and stubborn. But he loves very hard, and when he feels invested in you, he's never going to give up on you."

For some reason, I felt real comfortable around Wynner. Maybe it was because she basically told me her family's business or the fact that she had this cool vibe about her, but I felt like I could be honest with her about my life.

"I just don't want to waste my time on a man that's not going to be worth it. That's my biggest fear and why I haven't reached out since we hung out a few days ago."

"Parrish is a headache and will make you pull your hair out. So, I'm not about to lie because he's my brother. However, he's worth all the headache that he will give you. He's really a sweet person when he wants to be."

"I guess I can call him back and stop ignoring him. When is he going to give up?" Don't judge me because I was confused. Here I was, mad because Shaq wasn't persistent and didn't chase me like a man should. Yet, I had a man that hadn't let up since he saw me days ago, and I was complaining. Women, huh?

"What's the harm of you just giving him a chance? I usually wouldn't be too happy about it, but you met him first, so I can't be mad."

From her face, I could tell she was thinking about something. "Wynner, I like you. So, if something happens between me and your brother, trust that you and I will still hang out. I'm not that type of girl, and I hate girls that are like that." That was something that I had to run across her.

She was so used to those bird-ass hoes that wanted to befriend her for some dick. I loved dick like the next person; however, I wasn't about to act like someone's friend to get it. Even if Uzi and I didn't end up being anything, I would continue to come around and be her friend. Uzi was fine as hell, but not fine enough for me to fuck somebody over to be with him.

"You don't have to continue being friends with me," she told me. "I'm not going to be hurt or make you feel guilty."

"Wynner, I'm not gonna tell your ass again. You're basically stuck with me. Now that I know you live in the city, I'll hang out with you before or after work. . . . 'Cause I might need a place to sleep so I don't have to head to Staten Island."

She started laughing and put her glass down. "I'll run it past my husband and see what he says," she giggled. "I'm just kidding, you can come to hang anytime."

As I was about to respond, her phone rang. She rolled her eyes and answered. "Yes." She messed with her hair and placed her phone on speaker.

"You in the crib? Jah told me he left you to go handle business," Uzi's sexy-ass voice came through the line. Just hearing his voice made my panties superwet. This man had all types of swag.

"Yes, Parrish. . . . Guess who I'm with?" she snickered.

"Who? Qua still in Miami, and you ain't got no damn friends, so who the fuck you with?" From his voice, you could hear him getting agitated with the guessing game that Wynner was playing.

"First of all, you need to relax and stop being all hostile."

"Wyn, stop playing with me," he warned. "Who the hell you got in your crib?" he asked again, more sternly this time.

"Remi, Parrish. Remi came to hang out with me after the club. And Jah didn't go handle business. He went to chase after a girl."

"Now, why you use the word chase? You know that nigga ain't chasing shit," Uzi joked, and both Wynner and I cracked up laughing. "Word. I'm on my way over to your crib now."

"Uh, no. We're having a private moment right now. We'll talk to you another time."

"Yo, you better stop fucking playing with me, Wynner Marie," he told her before he ended the call.

"Girl, he 'bout to run his ass over here. I should hide when he comes, and you say that I left."

"Lord, he's going to choke the hell out of me," she giggled. "Let's do it," she finally agreed.

We sat, drank wine, and talked about stuff until we heard her buzzer ring. When the buzzer rang, I hopped over the couch and went to the back. I had no clue where I was going, but I turned right and walked into a room with a big stuffed animal and baby bouncer. Closing the door quietly, I placed my ear to the door and listened as best as I could. Seeing that Wynner was in the club drinking, I wondered what this baby room was about.

"Where she went?" I heard Uzi's voice and put my hand over my mouth to keep from laughing out loud.

"She said she had to head home." Wynner's voice was shaky. You could tell from the tone of her voice that she was trying hard to keep her laugh in.

"Why the hell you sound like that, Wyn?"

"I had a few too many drinks, Parrish."

"Yo, you was calling me Parrish when she was here?" he questioned, and the voices seemed to get louder.

"Uh, yeah. I always call you Parrish."

I heard bedroom doors being opened, so I opened the closet to try to hop in. Instead, I was introduced to diapers stacked inside with no place for me to squeeze in. The handle to the door turned, and I hopped behind the door, hoping he wouldn't see me. When the door opened, he pushed the door open so wide that it hit me, and I yelled out.

"What the fuck?" I heard his voice, and he peeked around the door and saw me standing there holding my stomach. The doorknob had hit me right in my stomach, which caused me to tilt forward.

"Surprise," I said in between the pain I felt in my stomach. "Do you always open doors like that?"

"Hell yeah. This one was acting all jittery and shit, so I'm thinking she cheating on her husband and shit," he revealed, and Wynner laughed.

"The hell, Parrish? Why the hell would you think that?"

He shrugged his shoulders and then walked closer to me. "My bad. Why you ain't been answering my calls? You got a nigga or something and lied to me?" He gently pulled me from behind the door.

"Damn, Parrish. . . . She's holding her stomach, and you're giving her twenty questions. Come on, Remi." Wynner grabbed my arm and pulled me farther into the house.

She opened the double doors, which led to her massive master bedroom. I didn't think you could get a room this big living in New York. There was a huge, tufted king-size bed in the middle of the room with a fluffy bed bench at the end of the bed. Wynner continued to pull me into her bathroom that was connected to the bedroom.

"Here, take some Tylenol, because he tossed that door back hard." She went into the medicine cabinet and poured two pills into her hand.

"She gonna be good. I'm gonna take her to my crib and make sure she's straight," Uzi said like I had agreed to go somewhere with his ass.

"What the hell? You just hit me with the door, and now you want to take care of me?"

"Y'all shouldn't have been playing. See what happens when y'all play games?" he said, leaning on the door and replying nonchalantly.

"Nobody told you to toss that damn door back like the Hulk," I replied as I walked past him with Wynner.

We all filed into the kitchen where Wynner handed me some ice wrapped in a paper towel.

"Damn, I bruised my future baby mama all up. My bad. Zaddy didn't mean it." He wrapped his arms around me and kissed my neck.

"If you don't get the hell away from me," I shoved him while laughing. "I'm good for now. I'll send my doctor's bill to you."

"I'd rather you send yourself wrapped up in a bow, naked as fuck." He flicked his tongue at me, and Wynner gagged.

"Parrish, you need a damn filter. Why the hell you popped over here? . . . Never mind." She stopped when she saw how Uzi was practically fucking me with his eyes.

My damn head was killing me, so I went and sat down on the couch and held the ice on my face.

"I'm really sorry, though. I didn't think you were behind the door when I was searching in there."

"It's all good. I know you didn't do it on purpose. I'm just gonna head home and rest, 'cause you got me fucked up over here."

"You can stay in my guest room if you would like," Wynner offered, which was sweet. If I stayed here, then her damn brother would be on me like a dog in heat.

"Thank you, but I have to work in the morning, so I'm gonna head home. Take my number down, and we'll hang out after I get off."

We exchanged numbers, and then I grabbed my purse.

"Let me drive you to your crib. You live in Staten, and it's gonna take you forever to get home on the train and shit."

Hell, my head was hurting so badly that I wasn't about to turn down the free ride, even if he was the nigga that did this in the first place. "Get home safe," Wynner called behind us as we walked down the hall.

Uzi held the door open for me, and I slid into the front seat of his Mercedes. On the inside, it looked like a damn spaceship with all the buttons and knobs. When he got into the driver's seat, he was on his phone and from his tone, I could tell he was handling business. I've lived in the hood all my life, so I knew when a man was mixed in the streets. He had money, jewelry, and expensive cars, so he wasn't about to convince me that he worked a regular and legal job.

"Bet. I'll get with you later this week, and we'll handle it." He finished up his conversation and dropped his phone in the cup holder. "My bad. I had to take that," Uzi apologized as he pulled out of the parking garage of Wynner's building.

"It's all good. The street calls."

His head whipped my direction quickly as we stopped at a red light. "Why speaking on shit that you don't know?"

"I'm not speaking on shit that I don't know. You think I'm dumb? Nigga, you're in the streets, and I could tell from the way everyone acts around you at the club."

"Don't know what you talking about, but I know you better watch that mouth."

"Parrish, don't get slapped in your own whip. You mad because I figured you out?"

He was quiet for most of the ride. Part of me wanted to apologize because we both got heated; then the other part knew I wasn't about to apologize. I planned to ask around the club and find out what his story was. When I went to work, I did what I had to do and left. You never caught me hanging around and gossiping like the other chicks in the club. Next time I went to work, I was going to make sure I asked about Mr. Uzi himself.

"You got a smart-ass mouth, I see."

"Glad you have 20/20 vision and can see that. By the way, I'm involved with someone." Shaq wasn't my nigga, but this nigga here got me so mad that I felt the need to tell him that.

"Oh, word? So, he wouldn't mind me dropping you off at home?"

"He might."

"You playing. I believe you fucking around with a nigga, but he ain't your nigga. You don't strike me as the type that would get in my whip if you had a nigga."

"I'm spoken for. We don't need to get into what kind of woman you take me for," I snapped because his ass was doing too much. "You probably got a bunch of chicks you fucking."

"Nah, I'm just fucking with one on and off," he admitted. His bluntness shocked the shit out of me. Niggas loved to act like they weren't with nobody when, in fact, they were.

"Oh."

We arrived in front of my building, and I pulled to open the door, but he hit the locks. "Why you trying to rush out so quickly?"

"I'm tired, and do I need to remind you that I work tomorrow?"

"Give me a kiss."

"Didn't I just tell you that I fuck with someone?"

"Give me a kiss," he continued like I hadn't said a word.

"My man wouldn't appreciate that."

Leaning over, he wrapped his arm around the back of my neck and pulled me closer to him. I sat there and allowed him to push his lips on to mine and kiss the hell out of me. My tongue had a mind of its own because I shoved my tongue into his mouth, and he accepted it and sucked on it hungrily. My pussy was tingling. The good Lord knew how much I wanted to invite him upstairs. If

I lived alone, we would already be upstairs fucking. Still, I had to think of Tweeti and my mother, although I knew she didn't give a damn.

Pulling back from him, I smiled. "Now, you gonna get me in trouble with my man."

"You ain't got no damn man. Stop fronting."

"I'm messing with someone."

"Okay, and so am I. . . . You with that nigga?"

"No."

"A'ight, so why you lying to me?" The way he cocked his head to the side and smirked made me want to jump his bones right here and now. "You tried to make me jealous, I see."

"You and your eyes. You see a lot of things, huh?"

"Hell yeah. You gonna come chill with me tomorrow?"

"I work tomorrow."

"You eventually get off, right?"

"Don't be a smart ass." I hit him on the arm. "Me and your sister are supposed to hang before I head to the club."

"So, let me chill with you after the club."

"Hmm, sounds like that could be a plan. Good night, Parrish," I mocked, and he slapped my ass as I climbed out of the car. "Don't be touching me."

"Yeah, a'ight," he chuckled and watched as I went into the building.

When I got into my apartment, I was surprised that I didn't see Tweeti sitting at the kitchen table with warm milk. Since we were children, she could never sleep through the night. When we were younger, she used to wake up screaming because she couldn't sleep. When we spent the night at our dad's house, he introduced her to warm milk, so ever since then, she warmed milk and sat at the kitchen table while staring into space. When I didn't see her there, I went to her bedroom and quietly opened the door. The first thing I saw was a wheelchair and smiled. Jah had his arm wrapped around her, and she was sleeping peacefully. Closing the door, I went down the hall to my bedroom and got ready for bed. With work tomorrow and this headache I was nursing, I knew I couldn't go to sleep just yet, so I decided I would lie in bed until sleep eventually found me, or this headache wore off. Whichever came first.

The sound of someone banging on my apartment door jolted me from my peaceful slumber. With drool dripping down the side of my face, I wiped it and got out of bed. Stretching as I walked out of my bedroom, I looked into Tweeti's room. She wasn't in there. My mother was probably too knocked out to even hear that someone was knocking on our door like they were crazy. When I walked past the cable box, the time read that it was eleven in the morning. I didn't have to be at work until two, so just know I was pissed that I couldn't lay my ass back down and sleep. When I looked out the peephole, I rolled my eyes so damn hard. This nigga, Shaq, was standing there. We hadn't called or spoken in a while, so what the hell did he want? If a nigga couldn't call and check on me, then that was a nigga I didn't need or want in my life. Opening the door, I leaned on it and stared at him. The nigga had the nerve to bring his son right along with him. Yeah, if I fell back before, I was about to fall all the way back from his ass.

"What's good, babe? You been real distant lately," he said as he walked into the apartment. His son followed behind him eating a bag of chips.

"I've been distant? Shaq, let's not start our conversation with the dumb shit."

"Dumb shit? Yo, why the attitude?"

Was he serious? I hadn't heard from him, and he was asking me what's with *my* attitude? Granted, I didn't give a shit about him staying gone. My issue was that if you were going to stay gone, then do just that.

"Because you're banging on my door at eleven in the morning. We don't break bread together, so I know it's not about money. So, why are you banging on my door like this?"

He smiled and pulled me close to him, kissing me on the neck. His kisses did nothing for me. Instead of him kissing on me, I was imagining Uzi sucking on my breast and neck. "I missed the shit out of you, ma." He kissed me again on the neck. "Give me some good shit." He pulled at my leggings like his son wasn't sitting right here.

"Your son is right here, Shaq. Fuck I look like?"

"The type to give your man some pussy." He continued to kiss me and make me feel gross. His son was just staring up at us, eating his chips. Yeah, he had to be no more than 3, but I felt like he was staring into my soul as his father tried to talk me into giving him some pussy.

"There you go with that word again."

"What word?"

"Man."

"I'm not your man now? Who the fuck got in your ear and got you acting funny?" Moving away from him, I grabbed some water out of the fridge and sat down at the kitchen table. If he really wanted to know, a nigga like Uzi McKnight got me all open and ready to hand him the panties on a silver platter.

"We were never together, Shaq. Fucking, smoking, and chilling occasionally isn't 'being together.'"

"You never corrected me before. I'm out here claiming you, and you over here got a nigga looking stupid."

"Nah, you got *yourself* looking stupid. I never gave you the impression that we were together, or would be together."

"You didn't? Screaming my name during sex ain't giving me the impression?"

This is how stupid this nigga was; he was over here professing his love and how he claimed me in the streets but had me mixed up with another chick. When Shaq and I fucked, I never screamed his damn name out. This nigga always left me pissed after we fucked, so I had to finish the damn job myself.

"You on your period or something?" As I was about to answer him, he cut me off and continued speaking. "I gotta make a run, so I need you to watch Sunjai."

"Eh, I don't fucking think so. Where the hell is his mama?"

"She got a doctor appointment for his little sister. Plus, she due any day now and 'bout to pop. He be running her to death, and she need to relax and shit."

Shaq had me all the way fucked up with everything he was saying. It wasn't just a few things he was saying; it was *everything* his ass said. This nigga low-key just told me that his baby mama was pregnant. Now, when I did my math, he and I had been messing around for at least a year, so he was fucking this chick the same time he was fucking around with me. Which is fine, but don't act like you been out here claiming me while being faithful. Meanwhile, you adding to your football team of damn kids.

"Shaq, get the hell out of my house and take your son with you. In here acting so butt hurt because I'm not claiming you, but out here getting everybody and their mama pregnant. Nope, it won't be me."

"Wow, you don't wanna have my kids?"

"Nigga, what? Did you *really* ask me that question?"

If I didn't get him out of my house, his son was going to be front and center for my own personal season premiere of *Snapped*. This poor baby had boogers all over his face mixed with chips, but his father was in here too pressed over some pussy.

"Yeah. You acting like having my seed is the worst thing in the world."

"It is. You got countless baby mamas and kids. I'm not trying to be added to that list." I was still flabbergasted that he even *asked* me that question. My life wasn't together, so what did I look like bringing a child into this world?

"Man, whatever. I'll ask his god-mama to watch him."

"You probably fucking her too," I added as I walked him to the door. He turned around and stole a kiss from my lips.

"Stop with all of that." He kissed me again. *Remi, move or slap him or something,* I tried to tell myself. Like a punk, I stood there and allowed him to kiss me. "I'm gonna come over tonight. You gonna be home?"

"Yeah."

He kissed me once more before he grabbed his son's arm and walked down the hallway.

Closing the door, I laughed because I was going to make sure I *wasn't* home. This nigga had another think coming if he thought he was about to fuck me, then get lost for a week. Nah, I had enough of his disappearing acts, so I needed a break from him for a while. Maybe I would just leave his ass alone for good. How do you break up with someone you're not with? These niggas these days were making it harder for us females. Now, I had to figure out a way to tell this nigga who *wasn't* my nigga, that he *ain't* my nigga no more. Tongue twister, right? I quickly made breakfast and got ready for work. The day needed to fly past quickly because I wasn't in the mood.

Qua

Being away from my wife was never easy for me. Still, bills needed to be paid, so I had to make sure that the money was always piling up. This was the third time that she miscarried, and you would think it would get easier to deal with; instead, the shit was harder than the time before. Wynner was so strong with everything else except this. I've watched her heart break each time they told us they couldn't hear a heartbeat, or she was bleeding because she had miscarried. I loved the shit out of my wife and in a perfect world, we would have a healthy baby in our home. Yet, it didn't take away from the love that I had for her. Wynner always cried about me blaming her for not being able to carry our baby. The shit pissed me off because I would never blame her for something that wasn't her fault. She did everything the doctors said, and it always seemed to happen.

Telling her that we should take a break on the baby stuff broke her heart. Shit, it broke mine to have to tell her that. I knew it was for her own good because she would continue to stress about getting pregnant again. Baby making was supposed to be easy and fun, and Wynner made the shit seem like a chemistry test. She had all these ovulation kits and took her temperature every morning and a whole bunch of other shit. For a few months, it would feel nice to take a break from talking about babies and just enjoy my wife. She had me eating all this crazy shit that helped build stronger sperm and shit. All I wanted was to fuck my wife and not have her lying in the bed with her legs above her head after we finish making love.

Each time she fell pregnant was a happy yet nervous time for us. Wynner got excited and would start shopping and filling the baby room with stuff. That room door stayed closed because each time she miscarried, it was too painful for her to see that room. I felt responsible for all of this because I was the one who told Wynner I was ready to start a family. I'm 31, and I felt like it was time to bring a child into the world with my wife. That was the one thing that was missing in our crib, and it was something I always wanted. When we first got married, I wanted kids. Still, I didn't want to have any because I was bringing in no money, so it would be irresponsible to bring a child into the world. Then, Wynner was only 20 and hadn't lived yet or did shit for herself. It wasn't fair for me to knock her up before she was able to do shit for herself. Granted, she didn't have friends when we got married, and she still had none. I wanted my wife to be happy and ready to have a baby, not because I wanted one. Sometimes, I felt like she did all of this just to make me happy, and although I appreciated it, that's not what I wanted for her.

The trip to Miami was quick, and I was on the plane back home before I knew it. As I walked through JFK airport, I couldn't wait to see Wynner's face when I walked into the crib. She was always home waiting for me, and since she didn't know I was coming home, she was going to be surprised. Tonight, I was going to take my beautiful wife out and wine and dine her. My baby was perfect for me, and I felt like I was the winner in this marriage. She didn't nag; she was patient and knew when I had to handle business and didn't bitch about it. Not to mention, she wasn't in everyone's club shaking her ass when I was out of town handling business.

The town car was waiting for me as I slipped into the backseat with my duffle bag. The driver smiled and pulled away from the curb. If there was one thing about Uzi, when he sent me to handle business, everything was top-notch. I flew first class, had town cars and luxurious hotels, all on his expense. This Miami trip didn't go how I planned. Uzi's homie wasn't feeling the numbers I had put down, so I was going back home with bad news for this nigga. He had been on my nerve, so I was going to hold off a few days and spend that time with my wife. After the whole miscarriage, I was kicking myself in the ass for having to handle business and not being there for her.

"Did you enjoy your stay, sir?"

"I never enjoy my stay when I'm handling business," I shot back as I checked my emails. Between working for Uzi and trying to get my own business off the ground, a nigga was tired.

Working for Uzi was never supposed to be something I did for the rest of my life. I didn't want to work for this nigga at all, but when he came to me about business, I was in a badass situation and needed money. Wynner and I had just got married, weren't living together, and I was sleeping on my homie's couch. So, when he came to me about making some money, I jumped on that shit with the quickness. It was something that I needed to do to make sure that Wynner was set for life. I knew this life didn't end well, and there were only two ways that it ended: either death or jail. Shit, I wasn't trying to do either, so I was making plans to secure my future without selling drugs for the rest of my life.

I'd been cutting hair since I was a teenager. The shit was in my blood since my father did the same shit before he bounced out of my life when I was 12. I had a cousin who had just come home and needed a job to keep him from joining the same life I was a part of. He had been begging me to put him on, and I kept ignoring him. The nigga did fifteen years in prison, and since he was the only family I had, his ass wasn't about to go back on my watch. It was crazy because he was older than I, and the only thing he knew was to hustle. The barbershop wasn't for him, but it was going to keep him off the streets and help me go legit. Then, I had been in talks about buying a gas station. There was a bunch of shit that needed to be done before I could do it, so I was sitting back and saving bread so I could buy it when the time came.

The traffic was normal, so it didn't take long before we pulled in front of my building. After saying my good-byes, I hopped out and walked inside of the building. It felt good as fuck to be home, and I couldn't wait to hold my baby in my arms. I knew Wynner like the back of my hand, and I knew she was sitting on the couch watching a movie and scrolling social media. It didn't matter how many times I pushed her to go out and find some friends her age, she never did. I'd rather have a homebody than a chick that was at every function; still, I felt like she need-ed more than just her family and me. Holding in all the shit we'd been going through wasn't good for my baby.

Soon as the elevator got to our floor, I rushed down the hall to our door. Unlocking the door, I set my bag near the foyer table and proceeded into the crib. When I made it to the living room, she wasn't there. Then, I went to the bedroom, and she wasn't there either. It made no sense to check the kitchen since our layout was an open floor plan. Checking the guest room and then the baby's room, I whipped my phone out and called her with the quickness. Other than her mama's house, where would she be?

"Hey, baby, what's going on?" she answered on the first ring. Her voice sounded . . . different. I half-expected her to be down and out, but she sounded chipper, like she had the best day ever.

"Where you at, Pooh?" For as long as I could remember, that was the nickname that I had given her. It stuck with us through all these years, so I liked to think it was good luck.

"Wait, are you home?"

"Yeah, and I'm wondering where my wife is?"

She giggled. "I drove to Harlem with my friend to pick up her check. I'll be home in a bit, okay?"

Friend? Who the hell was this friend? And apparently, this friend had a damn job because she was driving her to pick up a check. Wynner ain't never mentioned having a friend. Shit, she didn't have to mention having one because her actions showed me. Wynner didn't go out unless it was to lunch with her mama, or her brothers came over and decided to take her out to dinner. Then, there were times when we went out but did all that count as going out with friends?

"Who your friend?"

"Babe, what's with the twenty questions?"

"Shit, Wyn . . . I come home and find my hermit crab wife with no friends is out with a friend. This is new to me, so who your friend?"

"Her name is Remi. She's Uzi's friend. We'll talk when I get home, okay?"

If she was Uzi's friend, then he trusted her to be with the chick. I wanted to come home and lay up with my wife, yet she was out doing her. Part of me had more questions; then the other half knew this is what she needed. Wyn sounded like she was having a good time, and I'd rather that than have her down and thinking about the miscarriage she just suffered. Plopping down on the couch, I dialed my cousin's number. Since my wife was out and about, I guess I should go spend time with the only family I had.

Up until I turned 12, both my parents had been in my life. It wasn't until I turned 12 that they decided they didn't want to be parents anymore. My father bounced and left me with my mother. Then, she got tired of finding out what he was doing from the streets, so she dumped me off at some woman's house and never came back. The woman happened to be a friend of hers that owned a boy's orphanage, and she took me in. Growing up was hard as hell, and all I wanted was to have a better life. For the life of me, I couldn't understand why my parents didn't want me. Why wasn't I enough for them? My cousin, Grizz, was a few years older than I was; yet, he had been in prison his whole damn life. He went in when he was 18 for an armed robbery charge. Instead of snitching as he could have, he did fifteen years and missed out on life.

"What the fuck is up, nigga?" Grizz answered the phone extra hype as usual.

Even when the nigga was in prison, he still greeted me the same way. He had got out six months ago and was trying to change his life. When he came home, he tried to jump back into the streets to get money. Instead, I had him set up with a condo, car, and some money; yet, he wasn't satisfied sitting by and collecting money without earning it.

"Where the fuck you at?" I laughed at how hype he always was.

"Shit, I'm in the crib wondering where I'm 'bout to eat. . . . What's hitting over your way? Wait, ain't you in Miami?"

"Nah, I came back early after handling business. Remember when we had that talk?"

He chuckled. "How could I forget? You sat my grown ass down and told me to move smarter, not harder. Why?"

"That barbershop ain't gonna open itself. So, we need to grind and get this bread."

"A barbershop is not about to fund your life, kid. Your wife drives a custom Audi. Shit, you drive a damn Range Rover, so how the fuck a new barbershop is paying for that? Not to mention y'all crib you live in Greenwich Village. Wyn shops in stores that women dream to shop in, so you can have this backup plan, but don't put all your eggs in one basket. You said her brother been giving you more and more responsibility. Bring me on as your right hand and let's get this bread."

A lot of what Grizz was saying rang true. I was so focused on this barbershop that I didn't think of anything else. "You might be right."

"Nigga, I'm always right. I'm not saying not to start the shit. Let's start the shit, get some people to work and build it up but continue to hustle. How the fuck you gonna open a new shop and quit the game with all the expensive shit y'all got?"

"A'ight. I hear you, dammit."

"Do you, though? You need to be in Uzi's ear about taking over one of his boroughs. That nigga been slacking lately, and niggas are getting put on to game."

Uzi handled business when his heart was in it. Usually, it was he who made the trips to Miami; yet, he sent me. It showed me that he trusted me to handle business without him right there. Still, while he spent his money and enjoyed his life, his empire was being threatened by these new cats who felt they had something to prove.

"You right. And I do hear everything that you're saying. I'm gonna holla at him about it."

The last thing I wanted to do was speak to Uzi about business. I usually let him tell me what needed to be done, and I handled it. Our relationship was strained, so I never wanted to step on his toes and cause more stress for my wife. My life was about keeping a low profile and handling business so that my wife never had to want for anything. Wynner was spoiled when we met, so I wanted to keep her that way, even though she told me that I didn't need to.

"Look, let me come along and smooth the shit over. I'm a year older than him, and he might listen to a nigga like me."

"Age ain't got shit to do with it, bigheaded ass."

He laughed. "Yes, it does. You know I be schooling you niggas."

"Whatever . . . I'm gonna head over to his crib tomorrow, so let's link and handle this."

"Bet. You found me a shorty yet? I heard about the Usher shit and ain't trying to run up in just anything."

"Stay yo' ass off TMZ and do something productive."

"Soon as you have that conversation," he told me before we ended the call. Instead of sitting around, I went into the kitchen and grabbed some shit to cook. Being away had me missing my wife like crazy, so I wanted to cook dinner and show her how much I appreciated her.

The door chimed, and I heard a pair of heels clicking on the wooden floors. I didn't bother to move from the couch or pause the show that had been watching me for the past few hours. Looking at my Rolex I realized that it was after midnight, my ass leaned up quicker than I expected because I lost my balance. Wynner placed down two shopping bags by the kitchen island and smiled when her eyes landed on me. What could I say about the angel that I called my wife? Her smooth, vanilla-colored skin was always flawless. I mean, how the fuck you wake up and look put together? That was Wyn. She always was flawless, and it didn't matter what she did. Her slanted hazel eyes always reminded me of cat eyes. Even in the dark, they reflected and creeped my ass out sometimes. Then, her nose . . . Wynner hated her nose because she had her father's nose. It wasn't small; yet, it wasn't big. It was medium, and when she was upset, that shit flared like a muthafucka.

Just staring at her juicy-ass pouty lips had me wanting to suck on them. My baby was five foot two, and when she was pissed, she always wanted to act like she was six foot seven and try to punk my ass. Her body was amazing with a nice, plump ass, perky breasts, and a flat stomach. She was small from skinny; still, she was thick in all the right places. Right now, she was standing in front of me wearing her hair straight, just like I liked it. Part of me wished I could ignore the time she just walked her ass in here, but I couldn't.

"Baby, what are you still doing up?" she had the nerve to ask me like *I* was in the wrong. Shit, she knew why the fuck I was up.

"Wyn, where you coming from?" It didn't make sense to have all this small talk before I got to questioning her ass.

"Remi had to work, so I stayed at the club with her for a few. When Uzi showed up, he walked me to my car and told me to head home."

"So, I guess the phones didn't work in the club, huh?"

She giggled and walked over to me. Rubbing her hands up my chest, she stared up at me with that innocent pout on her face. "Shoot, I'm sorry about not calling. Time crept by me, and here we are now. Don't be mad." She rubbed my face.

"I'm not mad, more worried. Like, damn." I removed her hands from me and went into the kitchen.

She stood in the middle of the floor for a second, then followed me around the island into the kitchen. "Is all of this for me?" She pointed to the kitchen table set with our food that was now cold as shit.

"Was supposed to be. I'm going to bed. I'll have the cleaning lady clean it up in the morning." I excused myself to the bedroom. Wynner had called me, but I ignored her.

Yeah, I wanted my wife to have friends and go out instead of being in the crib all day. But I didn't want her in a strip club hanging with her friend. Niggas weren't going to be only looking at the bitches; they were going to try to get in her ear. Wynner wouldn't pay them any mind. It was the thought alone that pissed me the fuck off. She was my woman, and I didn't want niggas drooling over her like she didn't have a whole man at home waiting on her.

"Quamere Classon, I know you heard me calling you from the kitchen. What's going on with you?" She stood in the doorway with her hands on her hips.

"You in the fucking strip club around mad niggas. Since when the fuck did you think that shit was cool?"

"You go to the strip club all the time. Do I complain?" she shot back.

"Fuck you mean? We're not talking about what the fuck I do. We're talking about you."

"And I just asked a question, so answer it."

"Nah."

"So, the moment I'm out having a good time, you're tripping. For what? Do I ever go out and engage in conversation with other men? This ring is pretty big, and I have no problem waving it in front of another man's face to let him know I'm spoken for."

All these fucking pillows she had on the bed pissed me off. Wynner claimed it was for decorations, but when it came time to jump into bed, I had to peel each one off the bed until there were only four pillows left on the bed.

"I'm tired. You're home, and that's all I was worried about."

"Childish as hell, Quamere. I'll let you have your moment and sulk if that's what you want." She turned and walked out of the bedroom.

Starting an argument with Wynner was the last thing that I wanted to do. Since we couldn't have sex just yet, I wanted to massage my wife's naked body, kiss every inch of her, and lie in the bed with her while telling her how much she meant to me. Instead, I was fluffing these damn pillows and mumbling shit to myself while she turned on the TV in the living room. From the bedroom, I could hear *Love & Hip Hop*.

"Your ass wouldn't have to watch the recording if you was in the crib," I mumbled before I lay on the pillow and stared out the window.

Half of me wanted to sit in this bed and sulk because my wife came bouncing up in here at midnight. Then, the other half of me wanted to warm the food up, pull her close, and watch her ratchet TV show with her while she rubbed my head. Shit, that other part of me was silenced by the part that wanted to be near my wife. Pulling the covers back, I walked back to the front and found Wynner warming the food up herself.

"Sit down. I'll finish."

She stopped messing with the stove and glanced back at me. "Why you gotta do all of that? I'll finish warming it up."

Shrugging, she walked away from the stove and went to the back. Thirty minutes later, she came back with her robe pulled tight, and I had the plate set on the coffee table with her show paused. Next to her plate was a glass of wine and the remote.

"Is this your way of saying sorry?" She stood with her hand on her hip.

"Perhaps."

"Okay, DJ Khaled. I'll accept your apology under one condition."

"What's that?"

"Drop this jealousy thing you have, Qua. You've had it for years, and it was only quiet because I'm always under you. Tonight, for the first time, it came out, and I saw it all in your eyes. Green isn't your color."

"The shit makes me upset. You know how the fuck I feel about you, Wyn."

She walked over to me and pointed her freshly mani-cured finger in my face. "And you know how I feel about you. I'm not checking for another man at all. You're the only man that has my heart, so all that jealousy shit is not necessary."

"I got you."

"Okay, give me a kiss." She reached up, grabbed my face, and shoved her lips on to mine. Shit, this was the reason why she had my ass going crazy.

When I first started messing around with Wynner, it was a secret. We had to keep shit on the low from her brothers, so we did everything two cities over or places we knew her brothers would never frequent. Wynner McKnight had all the niggas around my way going crazy. Uzi's little sister, who was untouchable, had every nigga wanting her. When she would talk to other guys and smile, I would get upset. One summer, I remember she came out of the crib in some little-ass shorts. Uzi was away on business, and Jah was somewhere with some chick. I swear on my unborn kids that I wanted to run over and grab her ass up. She had niggas drooling as she walked past with some chicks she used to run with. It was then that I knew that she was the girl I wanted. No other chick had me doing shit like I did chasing Wynner around. If a chick had you jumping out of bushes and shit, then she was wifey material.

While Wynner got comfortable and engrossed in the show, I lay back on the couch and watched as she cackled at funny parts and rolled her eyes at some of the women she couldn't stand on the show. The reason I was so crazy over Wynner was because she wasn't like other women out there. There was only one woman that could make me feel the way I did, and that was her. Once she finished her food, she reached for me to lay on her lap. This was my favorite part of our nights when she watched TV, her rubbing my head and playing with my ears.

"You know I love you, right?" Staring up at her, she stared down at me with a smile on her face.

"Yes, I know how much you love me. Now, take yourself to sleep because I know that's what you're about to do."

Laughing, I lay back down on her lap and fell asleep just like she predicted. Wynner just had this calming scent about her that made me feel calm whenever I was near her. Yo, she was really my baby for real.

Uzi

The constant ringing of my damn bell was starting to piss me off. One of the damn maids needed to answer that shit and leave me the hell alone. Staring at my phone, it was nine in the damn morning. Once the ringing stopped, I put the pillow back over my head and got comfortable. Just as I was about to close my eyes, someone started knocking at my door. I didn't get in until around four this morning, and now I was being forced to get up and deal with whoever couldn't wait.

"What?" I barked.

"What? Man, you better answer me better than that," Clarise, my housekeeper, yelled back through the door. "You have visitors down in the formal living room." She sucked her teeth.

"Who the fuck is visiting?"

"Your brother-in-law. He's with another big man," she replied.

"A'ight. I'm coming."

Snatching the covers off, I grabbed some briefs out of the top drawer of my nightstand and put them on. After that, I grabbed my Versace robe from behind the door and tossed it on. A nigga loved sleeping in the nude. Nothing like feeling your dick pressed up against some soft and cold-ass silk. Clarise was still standing at my door when I swung open the double doors and stared at her. Right on time, she had my coffee in her hand with a donut. I paid good money to keep her around, so I expected her to always be on point.

"You said, big guy?" I sipped my hot-ass coffee and stared at her.

"Yes, he's really big. I have them in the formal living room with some refreshments," she told me and headed into my bedroom. "Are you going back to bed?"

"I have a feeling that I won't be tired after this impromptu meeting. Go ahead and clean my room." She went into the room, and then I remembered something. "Aye, what did your son get on his test?"

She walked over to me and smiled. "He got the passing grade that he needed." She smirked. "Appreciate it, rude ass," she snapped and went back into my bedroom.

Since both my parents were the only children, Clarise was the closest thing I had to a young and hip aunt. She worked in the corner store that my li'l niggas sold in front of. One night I stopped by to see how the money was flowing. I heard the owner of the store barking on her about coming into work late. After she explained to him that her son was in the hospital and she couldn't come into work that night, this nigga called her everything under the sun and kicked her out of the store when she asked to be paid early. Apparently, her rent was due, and she needed to pay that and get back to the hospital to be with her son. The shit had me so mad that I went into his store, put my gun to his face, and threatened his ass. All he gave her was a hundred dollars and claimed that was all she earned. Since I was done for the night, I offered to drive her home so she could pay her landlord, and then take her to the hospital.

When we pulled up to that crack shack, I knew I couldn't allow her to give that hundred dollars to the slum lord. My crib had just been finished, and I had the apartment in the basement. The only time I saw this woman was when I went to the store to get roll-up, or I happened to grab a sandwich there. Each time we crossed paths, she was always nice, funny, and sweet.

Now, I could have been wrong about her, and she ended up lining me up since she knew where I lived, except she turned out to be family to me. She and her son Clay turned out to be what made this crib not so lonely at times. Clarise had a mouth on her and let me have it, even if I was the nigga signing her checks.

"Tell him I got the money I promised him."

"Stop buying him, Uzi."

"Yeah yeah yeah." I waved her off and headed downstairs. After I passed the kitchen, I found Qua sitting in the living room, fucking up some donuts and coffee. He had another overly big nigga sitting beside him. This nigga looked like he could be a damn bodyguard. If he wasn't, he needed to be because he was a big-ass nigga.

"What's good, Uzi?" Qua stood up and dapped me. "This my cousin, Grizz," he introduced the giant.

"I'm all for family coming over and shit, but damn, why the fuck you here so early?"

Qua chuckled. "Business waits for no man. I had to holla at you about something and need to find out if you're down."

Sitting down in the armchair across from them, I finished the piping hot coffee and stared at them intensely. If there was one thing I was good at it, it was reading people. I was never wrong about a person. With Qua, though, I could never read this nigga, and he hasn't proven me wrong or right yet, so I didn't know where I stood with this man.

"What's this business you need to talk to me about?"

"Let me get Brooklyn."

"Brooklyn? Where this coming from?" Qua always did what needed to be done and never requested shit. He took whatever I said and did what needed to be done. This was the first that I was hearing of him wanting to take over one of the boroughs.

"I've been working with you for five years, doing all that I needed to do to provide for my wife. I'm tired of doing the scrap work, and I'm ready to put in some real work and bring on my own team."

"Who this big nigga?" I laughed, stood up, and dapped him. "Uzi," I introduced myself.

"What's good, man?"

Sitting back, I could see the hunger in Qua's face. This was something that he wanted, and for him to come early in the morning to discuss this, I knew he meant business. My team in Brooklyn had been slacking, and I hadn't put them in their place. Part of it was being busy, and then the other half was being too lazy to handle it.

"You can have it."

"Word?" Qua's face lit up. "Wait, what's the catch?"

"Deal with them niggas. Money has been coming up short, and you already know how that goes."

"Bet," Grizz spoke up. It didn't need to be said that he was bringing his cousin on as his right hand. Every nigga needed a right hand that was going to keep it real with them. Jah was mine, so it was only right that I allowed him to bring his cousin on.

"You good with the agreement?" By the look of Qua's face, he didn't sign up for all this shit.

Nodding his head, he stood up. "Yeah. If that's what needs to be done, then I'll handle it. Taking food from the family is a hell nah in my book."

"Handle business. Once that is handled, come holla at me, and I'll get you linked in with everything."

"Bet. That's what I wanna hear. I'll hit you tonight when that's all handled."

"Tonight?"

"I'm handling that shit tonight. Niggas stealing, so they gotta get dealt with," he said with a stone face.

"Well, a'ight, then. Let's get this money." I dapped hands with both of them again. When it came to Wynner, that the reason why I disliked Qua. However, when it came to handling business, that nigga did what he was supposed and made sure he handled business.

After they left, I went into the kitchen to pour myself some more coffee and pop another donut into my mouth. Instead of what should have been a moment of silence to myself, the front door opened and the sound of heels hitting my hardwood floors filled the house. It didn't take rocket science to tell me who just walked into my crib. Lira walked around the corner and had her hand propped on her wide-ass hips. For the life of me, I couldn't understand why she didn't get the hint that all I wanted to do was fuck. All that relationship shit we tried in the past, and the shit didn't work. Lira was holding on to something that we had in the past. Maybe I was part of the blame; she came to complain about us not being together, then I fucked her, so shorty probably was all confused.

"Why I gotta hear around the club that you're messing with Remi?" she scoffed as she stood there. Here she goes with the bullshit and what she had heard.

"I don't care if you heard I fuck dogs behind closed doors. Your ass need to start greeting people after running into their crib."

Sucking her teeth, she leaned on the island and rolled her eyes. "Good morning. Now, *why* am I hearing this?"

"Why you listening to the gossip of the club? How old are we? You running around here still listening to all this gossip and shit."

"Stop talking around it. Are you messing with her or not?"

"You looking real thick and shit." Ignoring her was the best thing to do in a situation like this. Lira would go on all day about this shit if I didn't distract her with some dick. I didn't lie, so I wasn't about to tell her that I wasn't messing with Remi. I didn't sit down and tell her directly that she was going to be my girl. We both knew where things were going to head; yet, we hadn't spoken on things yet. That kiss I gave her ass weakened her knees, and she wasn't even standing when I kissed her.

"Thank you. I've been working out trying to get this all together and stuff." She turned around in the tight-ass jeans she sported.

Lira was fine as fuck and knew she was beautiful. Her brown skin was so smooth and velvet. Her skin looked as if you could lick her cheek and taste some chocolate. Her oval-shaped eyes always appeared to be half-closed, yet she just had chinky-ass eyes. Her nose was small but had a small bump on the tip of it. She always complained about her nose since we were younger. Personally, it made her different. Lira was beautifully flawed. All her beauty was good to look at, but she had a lot of pain that made her the way she was.

"It's showing. I'm turned the fuck on." I licked my lips and pulled at my drawers.

Lira couldn't deny getting dick from me. She craved that shit and would probably lie on the stand for this dick. "We need to go to your bedroom."

See, she always had to fuck shit up. Since I moved into this crib, Lira had never been up to my bedroom. Each time we fucked, it was usually somewhere down here. Once, I let her sleep over in the guest room down here and made her believe it was my bedroom. When Clarise blew my spot up, she had been on me about going up there. My bedroom was my private space, and I didn't want to bring a chick who I'm just fucking up there. This crib was my home, and any chick that I got involved with had to move with me because I wasn't about to move.

With the money and time I spent here, I wasn't moving unless this shit was blown the fuck up. Even then, I might lie in my bed and get blown the fuck up with it. Some people had kids, but my crib was my baby.

"Nah, I want it right here," I growled and pulled at her jeans. Once her belt was unbuckled and her jeans were pulled down, I turned her around and pushed her head down onto the island.

Lira tooted that ass up and was ready for me to give her some dick. I stopped because I didn't have a condom. "Put it in," she begged.

She acted like I didn't know what she did in that back room. Hell, if she did anything close to other niggas that she did to me when I was back there, I needed this condom more than air. Lira wasn't a dirty person, and she took care of herself, but I also knew a lot of niggas had run in and out of her like the subway system.

"Stay right here," I growled, then slapped her ass. Speed-walking down the hallway, I dipped into the guest room and rummaged through the drawer. When I found one, I went back to the kitchen where she was still bent over waiting for this dick.

Opening the condom and slipping it on, I pushed inside of her. Lira's pussy wasn't as tight as it used to be. It was good pussy, just not as tight as I was used to. She was moaning, tossing her ass back and gripping the countertop, and I hadn't even done shit yet. Pushing the dick inside her was causing her to act all crazy and shit. Her back was arched, and if I wasn't about to dig all into this pussy, I would have been impressed. I held her hips and slammed my dick into her wet and awaiting pussy. Lira's gasps were so loud I was sure that Clarise heard them while cleaning my room. You had to be experienced to fuck the shit outta someone, put them out, and then continue drinking coffee when your housekeeper comes down.

"You like this shit? What was all that shit you were popping before?"

Lira's mouth was curved as she dug into the granite countertops. She couldn't find the words to speak back. I knew exactly what she needed to say, and she couldn't because this dick was feeling too good for her. "Nah, let me stop since you wanna be silent."

"Noooo, don't stop. I'm sorry, Uzzzzzzi," she moaned as I pulled her hair back and stared into her eyes. "I be tripping, daddy. What we got can't be broken or messed with," she added that last part.

Lira liked to talk this shit and think I agreed with it. To me, we didn't have shit, and if we did that, shit had been broken when she stepped her ass on that pole years ago. For the life of me, I couldn't understand why the fuck she was still stripping. Lira was 29 and was still throwing that ass in a circle for some crumpled up dollars. Then, if stripping wasn't enough, her ass was always in the back room doing the most. How she looked herself in the mirror at the end of the night was beyond me.

"I'm 'bout to nut. Come with me," I demanded, and she did as she was told. We both came right there in the kitchen.

Quickly taking the condom off, I tossed it in the trash and pulled my drawers back up. Lira was buckling her jeans up and fixing herself. We stood there staring at each other for a second before she decided to speak.

"Let's do lunch or something, Uzi."

"Nah, I got business to handle. I would still be asleep if Qua didn't come by and wake my ass up."

"Maybe I should hit Wynner up and do something," she pondered.

"Leave Wynner where the hell she at. Why you trying to hang with her?" She only wanted to get close to Wynner because she knew that was where my heart was. She and

I would never be, so she needed to stop trying to get close to my family like we would be one happy couple. Too much shit had happened, and a nigga never forgets.

"Eeew, why you acting like that?" she snapped. "Me and Wynner actually get along and like hanging out."

Wynner didn't dislike Lira; she just didn't want to hang around her. Lira tried too hard and was always hyping Wynner up, like she needed it. My sister knew she was beautiful, fly, and one of the most desired women in the city. She didn't need Lira to hype her up because she thought that it might get her a chance to be back with me. Shit, I didn't even know why I still fucked her or allowed her to show up at my crib. At this point, I was the dumb ass doing this to myself. Instead of fucking, I should have sent her on her way as soon as she came in the crib with her bullshit. The dick wanted what it wanted, right? How would I look turning down free pussy?

"She busy."

I smiled to myself when she followed behind me. Little did she know, she was being walked to the front door.

"Okay, but she's not going to be busy forever. I'm going to call her and see if she wants to hang out."

It happened so fast that she squealed. Putting my hand around her neck, I stared into her eyes and tried to read them. It seemed like she was scared, turned on, and upset—all in one. "I told you what the fuck it was. Stay the fuck away from Wynner and go on about your life. I'm not gonna keep reminding you about trying to push your way into my family's life."

"You act like it was only me, Parrish." Tears fell down her cheeks. "You didn't protest," she added.

Letting go of her, I glared at her. "Get the fuck on, Lira. Always talking that mess."

"You blame me so badly when you're as much to blame too," she spoke about some shit that had happened in the past.

"Lira, get the fuck on. I'll holla." I closed the door and went upstairs to my bedroom. Clarise was sitting in the sitting area watching Wendy Williams when I came into my room. Throwing myself on the bed, I closed my eyes.

"Stop letting her come in here and you wouldn't need to nap after she leaves," she told me, not bothering to take her eyes off the TV.

The Lord knew I loved my mama more than life, but she didn't get me. It was like she couldn't understand that I was a grown-ass man and had grown problems. With Clarise, she understood I was grown and didn't judge me for the mistakes that I had made. There was a lot that I had shared with her instead of my mother. Not to mention, my parents were living their life and not thinking about us. When it came to Wynner, they dropped everything, but with Jah and me, they kind of let us do our thing and didn't bother us too much. I could almost set my clock to when my mama wanted to do her usual pop-in to see if I was all right and alive.

"I'll learn one day."

"You should have learned . . ." she let her voice trail off. "Uzi, you're grown and will make your own choices. Just watch that woman because she's a mess."

"Appreciate it, Clarise." I winked, and she smiled.

"Always. Get you some sleep." she smiled and closed my bedroom door.

Stripping down, I went to shower and then climbed into my bed, butt-ass naked.

Tweeti

"If you call me one more time, I'm going to block you," I whispered in the bathroom at a restaurant. Jah's ass continued to call my phone like he had lost his damn mind.

"Why the fuck you not answering my calls then? You got me acting like I hit the pussy or something, Tweet." His voice was real calm . . . like a damn serial killer.

"I'm out on a date. I promise I'll call when I get home."

"A fucking date, with fuck boy?"

"Why you gotta do all of this?"

"Nah, bet." He ended the call, and I stood in the bathroom, staring at the phone.

There was something different that I liked about Jah; still, it didn't mean I had to stop dating just because he spent the night at my house the other night. Oaks called me and told me he wanted to take me to a movie and dinner. It was odd that he wanted to go all the way to Jersey instead of going somewhere in the city. Still, I didn't question it and just took the ride to have a good night.

"You good?" Oaks questioned when I came out of the bathroom.

"Yeah. It was my sister calling me to ask me something." It was a lie, and he could tell I was lying from the look he gave me.

"Who you fucking with, and don't lie to me," he laughed.

"We're not together, so I'm free to mess with whoever. Why you so concerned?"

"I'm not concerned. You the one getting all mad. I'm chilling." There was something about the way he said it that pissed me off.

Cutting into my steak, I took a bite and rolled my eyes. There was no need to make a scene with this nigga in this nice-ass restaurant. "Enjoying your food?" Switching the subject was the best thing I could do to avoid going off on him.

"Yeah, it was straight. You ready?"

"Damn, can I finish my fucking meal?"

"Hell, I thought you would have been finished by now." He sighed and leaned back in his chair like he had some-where to be.

"Are we even going to the movies?"

"Nah, my niggas need me back on the block," he re-sponded. Just like he knew I was lying, I could tell that he was lying to me too.

"So, where am I supposed to go? Home?"

"Nah, I'm gonna drop you off at my crib and come back when I'm done with them," he explained like this was cool with me.

"Did you ask if I wanted to come to your crib?"

"Shut up, you know you wanna continue to chill with me." He pinched my cheek and laughed. Even with a straight face, I still couldn't hold it in and ended up sharing a laugh with him.

Oaks was so much in a rush that I couldn't even finish my food. He had the waitress pack it up in doggie bag so we could hurry up and leave. As we rode back to the city, he spoke on the phone the entire time and acted as if he were just hanging alone. It pissed me off that he didn't mention that he was on a date and that his friends were actually interrupting us. Instead, he acted like he was chilling when they called and wasn't doing anything. Since my mother was having her spades night at the house, the last place I wanted to go was home right now, so I sucked up my feelings.

It didn't take us long to arrive at his house. Oaks lived on a little dead-end block in Queens. The shit was still the hood, no matter how much he tried to convince me there were white people on his block. The nigga acted like white people didn't live in the damn hood, collect food stamps, and all the other shit they loved to pin on us black folks. If you lived in New York City and had a corner store on the corner of your block, you lived in the hood. There was no other way around it. You lived in the damn hood. He parked in his driveway, hopped out, and ran up the three steps in front before I got out of this low-ass car.

By the time I got to the front of the house, he was already coming down the steps with a bag in his hand. "Go inside. My room is upstairs on the right, I'll be back fast as I can." He kissed me on the cheek and jumped into his car.

This nigga left me here at his house like I've been here before. With my purse and food container, I headed into the house. On the couch was another man watching ESPN. He smiled when he saw me standing there.

"Come in. Don't act all shy." He laughed and stood up. "Corey. I'm Oaks's roommate," he introduced himself to me.

Oaks liked to pride himself on being this street dude, yet he was sharing a house with a man who had textbooks scattered all over the table. Don't get me wrong, this man had tattoos and was fine as hell; still, he obviously wasn't in the streets like his roommate was. Or, maybe he was. Nothing surprised me these days.

"Tweeti. How are you?" I smiled. "Oaks's room is where?" The nigga was speaking so fast that I forgot what the hell he had told me.

"Yeah. You don't have to sit in his room. The nigga don't even have a TV. Come sit on the couch and watch what you want. I'm studying for this calculus test tomorrow anyway." He went into the kitchen. "Want something to drink? Grab the remote." His fine ass was a little pushy, but he was nice, so I smiled and did what he told me to.

Soon as I grabbed the remote, I put on my *House Hunters,* and he did a loud-ass laugh that caused me to jump. "You good?" The way he laughed had me turned around to make sure this nigga didn't break a voice box or something.

"Yeah, I'm good. It's funny because this shit is my show too."

"Really? People on here complain about the dumbest shit. I live in the hood and would take the dumb countertops that aren't marble and the carpet they're always complaining about."

"Word," he agreed and handed me a glass of water.

"How did you and Oaks meet?"

"We've been best friends since high school. The nigga been there through most of my hardest times." He sat down and popped open a beer.

"Nice. It's rare you find friends like that."

"Exactly. Most days, we're good; then again, he's in the streets, and you know how that goes."

"Let me guess . . . You don't approve."

"Nah. He's smart as hell and can do the same thing that I'm doing. We both saw what happened to my pops when he called himself being in the streets."

"The streets owe no loyalty to anybody. Maybe you'll rub off on him."

"Shit, if I haven't rubbed off by now, I ain't rubbing off on him. I'm about to graduate in a few months, and we've lived together since I started college."

"Damn. All you can do is worry about yourself. He's your friend, and I'm sure you love him, but he has to want better for himself. You can't be the only one who wants it for him."

"You right. Shit, how much you charge because you just made hella sense to me," he joked. "Let me go do these dishes. Call me if you need anything."

"Okay."

It had been three hours since Oaks dropped me off and dipped on out. Corey had grabbed his books and went up to his bedroom, and here I was, still sitting on this lumpy couch dozing off. I waited for another hour before I got my ass up and decided to sleep in his bedroom. His ass better have a good explanation of why he hadn't brought himself back into this house. Business calls, I understood that; yet, him not giving me a call and warning me pissed me off. When I made it upstairs, Corey's room door was cracked open. I figured I would tell him good night but stopped when I heard him talking to Oaks on the phone, and the phone was on speaker.

"You can't just leave her in the crib while you go to Atlantic City. That's foul, Oaks," Corey complained.

"Nigga, I'd be damn if I leave these baddies to come and drop her home. You need to drive because I would do it for you."

"I don't drive, and you have this woman here like she probably didn't have shit she needed to do. She came here to hang with you, I'm sure. You wilding, bro. And why you didn't tell me you were dating?"

"Nigga," Oaks laughed real loud, "who said anything about dating? Shorty fly, but she only good for fucking behind closed doors. Nobody gotta know that we're fucking."

"'Cause she big?"

"You know our friends would clown the shit out of my ass."

Moving away from the door, my heart started to beat faster and faster. I was pissed that this nigga was playing me. Yeah, I just wanted whatever bread he offered me, but after hanging out, I thought we could possibly lead to something. Hearing that I was good enough to fuck, but not flaunt around his friends hurt me. What made me so different from one of those skinny chicks I'm sure he was hanging with right now? Here I was, standing in the hallway shaking and wanting to grab the phone from Corey and curse Oaks the hell out. Instead, I calmed down and continued to listen.

"It doesn't matter what they would say. If she's wifey material, then you set that shit straight."

"Nigga, you don't have to deal with this shit because your girl fine as fuck." He had the nerve to comment on his best friend's girl.

"Oaks, you know I love you like a brother, bro. If you mention anything that has to do with my girl again, then we're gonna have a problem."

"Chill, you know I'm fucking with you. I'm gonna be there in the morning because these bitches changed their mind and want to go back to their crib. Her boyfriend works nights, so I got to be out in the morning, so I'll be there tomorrow morning. Just tell her I got caught up."

Once I heard that, I didn't wait to hear what Corey said. I went into Oaks's room and sat on his bed. Even his bed looked like a bed of damn lies. Oaks had me fucked up if he thought I was the type of chick that took shit and let it go.

Corey knocked on the door and cracked it opened. He offered a weak smile before he spoke.

"Oaks got held up, so he's gonna be here in the morning." He wasn't a good liar, so even if I hadn't heard everything for myself, I could tell that he was lying right through his teeth.

"Okay. I'll get some sleep then, I guess."

"Yeah, I'm so sorry about this," he apologized for his friend's fucked-up view. "Have a good night."

"You too," I smiled. Setting my alarm, I lay across the bed and closed my eyes with a smile again. Oaks had me all the way fucked up.

"Shit, keep stroking that shit like that," Corey moaned as I jerked him off with a smile on his face.

When my alarm woke me up, I crept in his room and under his covers, ready. See, I could tell that Corey wanted to fuck me, even though he had a girlfriend. When I first walked into the house, he looked surprised, then pleased, even when he closed the door last night after apologizing for Oaks being a dick. I knew from the way he eyed me down while sitting on the edge of the bed with my thigh exposed from the slit in my dress.

"Shiiiiit." His eyes popped open, and he sat up. "Tweeti, what the hell?" He pulled the covers back and jumped out of the bed with his drawers down and all.

Still in the bed, I smirked because there was no way that he was about to tell me to leave his room, especially not after that nut he had building at the tip of dick. "Let me finish," I cooed.

Corey pulled his underwear up and paced the small walkway from his bed to the door. "I can't do this. . . . You're my homie's girl."

"We're not together . . . and I just wanna make you feel good. From how stiff you are, I can tell you haven't busted a nut in a while."

"Shit, my girl wants to be celibate until we're married. The shit killing me, literally." His voice cracked just speaking about it.

"How about I take care of you, and this will be our little secret." I stood up and allowed my maxidress to drop down to the floor. "We don't have to tell a soul, and you can continue being a good boyfriend to your girlfriend." I unstrapped my bra and then pulled my panties down.

"Shiiiiit, you not playing fair." He licked his lips. From his eyes, I could tell he was turned on from what he saw. "Fuck it." He gave in and pulled his underwear down and damn near tossed me on the bed.

I was impressed by his strength. Soon as he got me on the bed, he spread my legs as he dug into his top drawer. After shoving shit around with his right hand, he found a condom and opened the shit with his teeth. Pussy must have been the best shit for this nigga because he was like an expert as he opened the condom and put the shit on with one hand. Soon as that condom was on, he pushed that shit inside, and I moaned. Now, this was supposed to be payback, but why did this feel so good? I wasn't supposed to be into this sex, but I was. This man had me moaning as he fucked the shit out of me. Corey pounded the shit out of my pussy so hard that I had to grab hold of the headboard and say a silent prayer for my lips.

"Fuuuuck." He leaned on the headboard with one hand and held on to my waist with the other one. "Shit feel so damn goooood!" he growled as I moved my hips to match his speed.

My little hips moving was no match for how beast this man was going. His girl needed to give him some pussy, or their wedding day may be a damn bloodbath. He might fuck her pussy clean off her body the night of their wedding.

"Flip over," he demanded, and I did what I was told. He slid right inside of me and continued to fuck the shit of me. His grip on my hips was tight as he banged into me like a screen door when it flies open in a storm.

"Right there." I slapped my hand over my mouth when that slipped out. Hell, I had to get over Oaks and enjoy this dick-down his best friend was delivering to me.

"You like that shit, huh? I wanted to fuck the shit outta you since you walked through the door," he growled in my ear and placed a kiss on it afterward.

Corey flipped and flopped me in all types of positions and didn't stop. We used five condoms because this nigga stayed hard. His dick would *not* go down, and I wasn't complaining. We were into our sixth session when his bedroom door suddenly slammed open, and we both jumped. I knew this is what I wanted, yet the shit still scared me because I forgot all about Oaks and was fucking the shit outta Corey.

"Yo, you dead ass, my nigga." Oaks's voice boomed through the room.

Corey jumped up with the quickness and grabbed his drawers off the floor. He didn't even put them on; he just held them in front of that monsta' he called a dick. Me, I climbed off the bed and grabbed my dress while Oaks tried to find the words to speak. By the time he found the words, my dress was on, and I held my bra and underwear in my hand.

"You a slut-ass bitch, for real." He tried to come at me with harsh words, and they did nothing to me.

"One, I'm not a ho. Two, you thought you were 'bout to fuck the 'fat bitch' behind closed doors and freak your other hoes in public. . . . Is *that* why you took me all the way to Jersey for a date?"

"Who the fuck told you that shit?" He eyed Corey, who shrugged his shoulders. "The real issue is you in here fucking my nigga with your fat, nasty ass."

"Aah, the real Oaks comes out," I giggled. "I may be big, and that's fine. I wear it well, and your best friend wanted to fuck me since I walked in the door. So, being big has nothing to do with it." I took a few steps toward him.

"Nah, you nasty as fuck. . . . Look at your body."

"Cute. Now, you're trying to body shame me? Wasn't you begging to eat my pussy on our way to dinner last night?" Pushing past him, I went into his room to grab my purse.

"I'ma deal with you when I'm done," he told Corey and closed his door. A few seconds later, he was closing his door behind him.

"If you try something stupid, I have mace and will not hesitate to use the whole bottle," I said, gripping my bottle through my purse. I was prepared.

"Why you do me like that?" he whispered like he wasn't coming at me crazy in the next room.

"Doing you like what? How you tried to do me, nigga?" As he stood there dumbfounded, I locked down an Uber and watched as it came to my location. It was five minutes away, and that was enough time for me to put him in his place and beat it outside.

"How'd I try to do you?" He acted like he didn't say a bunch of foul shit a few seconds ago, and then to add the shit he said last night to Corey.

"Tell Corey not to put his phone on speaker when studying. I heard about you wanting to fuck me 'in private.' Look, you like bigger women, and you think your friends are gonna punk you. Let's start with what type of grown-ass niggas punk women based on their size. What, are we in elementary school?"

"My bad. I don't know how to handle shit like this. My niggas are immature and shit." He tried to cop the plea after calling me everything except a child of God.

"Even if I wanted to accept your apology, I got too much respect for myself to fuck with you. Now, y'all be good and deal with the fact that Corey got to fuck this tight pussy before you." I winked and opened the door to leave.

"My bad, Tweeti." Corey was standing there with his robe wrapped around him. I didn't know why he was apologizing, but I smiled and walked to the stairs.

"You're good, love. I hope you ace that test today." With that, I headed downstairs and out of the house.

My ride was waiting there in front, so I jumped inside and dialed my sister's number on the way home. She wouldn't believe what the fuck went down. Oaks fucked with the wrong big girl. Don't get me wrong. There are some women who would have heard all the shit he was speaking and *still* waited for him. I'm *not* one of those women, and would never be one of those women. My mind went to Jah and what he was doing. Last night, he ended the call on me and never reached out again. After I showered and chilled, I was going to call him and see what he was doing today.

Remi

After a long day of work, I walked into our apartment and set our bags down on the console table. Keyshia Cole's old songs could be heard from the hallway, and Tweeti was singing her heart out. When I came around the corner, she was signing her heart out while holding a bottle of gin in her hand. This girl was hitting all the notes and swaying her hips from side to side like she had been cheated on recently. For a minute, I just stood there and watched her sing the hell out of this song as if she wrote it.

"I shoulda cheated on you!" She sang, in my opinion, one of Keyshia's best songs.

Turning down the radio, I stared at my dramatic little sister. She took being extra to another level. This girl had tears coming down her face as if she had really been cheated on. I had no words for the level of dramatics she had up her sleeve.

"Tweet, you know I could hear you downstairs," I told her as she turned down the music while sniffling.

"I gave him my best years. That nigga took my youth, and he gonna do me like that? He gonna cheat on me. I gave him everything." She cried with real tears coming down her damn face.

Here I was, standing in the middle of my living room, confused. When she called me at work, she told me a completely different story to the one that she was standing here telling me now. I knew for a fact that she and Oaks had only been talking a short while, so how the hell did he take her "youth"? Then, the fact that she was screaming he cheated on her confused me as well. Living with Tweeti, you never knew what was going through that dramatic-ass head of hers.

"Umm, Tweet, you know I love you, right? You cheated on Oaks, honey. You told me he walked into his house to you in bed with his best friend," I had to remind her crazy ass.

Her face changed, and then she laughed. "Damn, girl . . . The Uber driver was playing a bunch of Keyshia Cole songs. I came home and started blasting her songs, and next thing you know, I cracked opened this bottle of gin." She placed the bottle down on the table and then wiped her face. "That's talent right there. Keyshia need to get off *Love & Hip Hop* and make music like this again. Whew!" she laughed.

"You know what? I can't stand ya ass." We both laughed because the two of us knew how crazy her ass was. "Now, why did you do Oaks that way? I thought y'all were vibing and stuff."

"We was . . . until I heard him on the phone talking about I'm good for fucking behind 'closed doors.' He doesn't wanna parade me around his little friends, but he wanna fuck me. I think the fuck not." She went into the kitchen and grabbed some container out of the fridge, then tossed it in the microwave.

"Seriously? You're so beautiful, Tweet."

"Sis, I already know that. . . . I'm fly as fuck. Fuck what he thought. Now, his best friend wanna parade me around after the pussy he had this morning. Don't play with Tweet. Go play with your mama," she snapped her fingers.

"What's going on with Jah?"

Sucking her teeth, she took a seat at the kitchen table. "He was calling me like crazy last night, and I snapped on him. I was trying to get to know Oaks, and he was blowing my phone up."

"Tweet, why?"

"Girl, I was on a damn date. How rude of me to keep picking up my phone for his ass."

Shaking my head, I started messing with the salt and pepper shakers. "He seems like a good guy. You should at least give him a chance." There was something about Tweeti sleeping through the night the night he spent over here.

Even when she told me about the other men she messed around with, she was always up going through their house in the middle of the night. That night Jah spent the night, she slept the entire night, and she couldn't deny that there was something special about him. No, I didn't expect her to go off one night, but there could be something there.

"I'm sure he is. Homie just needs to chill." She grabbed her food out of the microwave and took a seat again. "You and Uzi? You haven't mentioned anything about him."

"Besides the kiss, we haven't hung out. He's busy, and I got work, so we keep missing each other."

"I don't know how you do it, Rem. Working all morning and then going to Harlem and working all night. You are my hero."

"You so stupid. Come out tonight and hang with me at the bar. I'll invite Wynner too, and you can meet her."

"Uzi's sister?"

"Yeah, she's really cool. We hung out the other day, and she took me to get my check. Girl, we ordered one drink and ended up in the bar way after I was off. Joey was happy because I was still behind the bar helping out."

"You mean, so if you like her, then I'll probably like her too." She reluctantly agreed. "After the day I had, I need me a few free drinks on the house. Joey's ass better not start about me working at the club."

"He has been asking about you too," I revealed. Joey thought it would be a good look for Tweeti to work behind the bar too. He said he wanted to see more curves behind the bar besides me. Tweeti claimed Joey gave her the creeps and refused to work at the club. Although she needed a damn job, she was stubborn and wanted to do things her way.

"Y'all so damn loud in here." The sound of my mother's slippers sliding across the floor greeted us before she did. "I like that hair on you, Tweet-Tweet."

"Thank you, Evelyn boo." Tweeti smiled as she chewed her food. "How was the game last night?"

"Listen, remind me not to invite those assholes over again. They got too damn drunk and tried to fight each other."

"Oh, hell. Last time they broke the kitchen table," I added.

"Uh-huh. I told them they better plan that shit over at their house next time. Anyway, what's going on with you girls?" She took a seat after pouring some soda.

"Work work work work," I sang Rihanna's hit song and gyrated my hips.

"The only gyrating you better be doing is right here and not up at the pole of the club," my mother sternly replied. "With all those tattoos on your body, I know they want you up there."

"Mommy, I'm not thinking about stripping."

"Good . . . What about you, Tweet-Tweet?"

"Trying to find a decent man to take care of me." My mother chuckled, then stopped when she realized that Tweeti was serious.

"Girl, take care of your damn self and don't worry about a man. Who was that man in the wheelchair the other morning?"

"A friend."

"That spent the night? When did you get male friends that stay the night?"

"He's just a friend, Evelyn. Plus, he's probably pissed at me or something." My mother shook her head and finished her soda. "I didn't speak to him much, but when he greeted me with 'ma'am,' I knew he ain't like other dudes. Does it bother you that he's in a wheelchair?"

"No, I don't see none of that. He's fine as fuck and got a big dick," Tweet let the last part slip out.

"Y'all fucked?" I blurted.

"No, he woke up with a stiffy and that shit was big and in charge. His legs don't work, but that dick do."

"Where the hell did I go wrong with you two?"

"Being a freak ho with our daddy." Tweeti started twerking, and it caused all of us to start laughing.

"The good Lord knows your daddy had some good dick." She fanned herself with her hands. "Speaking of him, where he been?"

"With his new wife. You know they eloped without us?"

My mother stared at me as I pouted and shook her head.

"You actually like his new wife?"

"She's all right."

"Don't try to downplay it for her, Rem. Yes, we like her, and she's very nice. Ev, you can't try to bully us into not liking our dad's girlfriend like when we were younger."

"That's not what I'm trying to do." She tried to convince us like she did when we were smaller.

Once we were older, my father started taking more time for himself. He started dating and getting to know women. When he brought his now wife around us, we didn't know what to think or feel. For years, my mother made us hate his girlfriends. We were older now, and we actually loved Rebecca. She was a white woman and had a lot to learn about having black stepdaughters, but still, she was cool. Most important, my father never stopped smiling when she was around him.

"Why y'all gotta ruin something, huh?" she snapped at us and got up from the table. "He's happy, and I'm happy for his gutta ass."

"Oh, I thought she was about to pull an Iyanla and call him a gutta rat," Tweeti chuckled, and I fell out in the chair laughing. My mother rolled her eyes and slid her ass back to her bedroom.

"She'll get over it."

"You trying to convince yourself, not me. She has no choice but to get over it. Daddy raised us and put his entire life on hold. Yes, Mama was there . . . but barely. He moved the hell on, and she needs to get clean and do the same with her man."

"I'm going to shower and get ready for tonight. I earned some good tips the other night, so I'm gonna take a cab there."

"Shit, how much that's gonna cost?"

"I don't know, but I'm not about to travel on the damn boat and train."

Just as I was about to head to my bedroom and change, someone knocked on the door. Tweeti stared at the door and then continued eating her food like she wasn't the closest to it. Ignoring her, I peeked through the peephole and opened the door for Sundae.

"You got some nerve coming over here," Tweeti raised her voice, apparently still mad about what Sundae did to her hair.

"I came over to apologize. Can't a girl miss her friends?"

Sundae was sweet and had been our neighbor for as long as I could remember. She was the same age as Tweeti, so they naturally gravitated toward each other. The thing you had to get used to with their relationship is the fact that they bickered like two old women. They could never agree on anything and constantly were at each other's throats. After Tweeti came home looking like Shirley Temple, they didn't talk for a bit until the other was ready to finally talk.

"It's crazy how you always got your hair laid, but you did mine so fucking wrong, Sundae," Tweeti continued to scold her.

"That weave looks bomb on you. I love the blond."

"Bitch, this is a damn wig," she retorted and rolled her eyes. "And if it wasn't for my homegirl in Harlem, I would have been with my short haircut."

"Oh, so you wanna talk shit about haircutting skills now?"

Tweeti turned and smiled at me.

"No, my damn head was cold with that shit. We're about to go into October. You know New York weather isn't one to play with."

"Yeah yeah yeah. Sundae, we're going to the club tonight, you down?"

"Only if Tweeti accepts my apology."

Tweeti turned her face up and then smiled. "Do me like you did again, and I promise, I'll beat your ass."

Sundae smiled and ran over to Tweeti to hug her. "Y'all crazy. I'm going to get dressed."

While I was in the tub, my mind drifted to Uzi and the last time we were together. When he kissed me, I felt tingles throughout my body. There was something different about him, and I couldn't lie and say I didn't want to know more about him. It was the way that he carried himself that had me all ready to toss my panties at him. We didn't spend hardly any time together because I had a life, and he had a life. Uzi thought I was stupid and didn't know he was in the streets. All I had to do was ask around about him, and that's what I planned to do at the club tonight.

"Damn, how long you going to take?" Tweeti busted into the bathroom to brush her teeth. She and my mother had no shame when it came to coming into the bathroom when I was using it.

"I'm finishing now. All I have to do is throw on some sweats and change at the club."

"Well, I'm getting dressed, and Sundae got a rental."

"Yass, so I don't need to waste money on an Uber."

"Yep. Hurry up."

It didn't take us long to get ready and head to the club. Sundae claimed she got the rental to head upstate to see some nigga she was messing with that was locked up. She was always writing some nigga that was on lockdown looking for love. The only thing she ended up finding was a man that wanted money on his books, a warm body in the chair during visitation, and someone to write him to help pass his time. Each time she got her hopes up, but when the nigga was released, they never reached out to her. One man came home and fucked her one night . . . then acted like he didn't know her when she ran into him with his wife in the mall.

"What's the move on after the club?" Sundae yelled over the music.

"Let's see where the night goes," Tweeti replied as she fixed her makeup in the mirror. She adjusted her gold grills in her mouth, then winked. "Damn, I'm fine as fuck."

Staring down at my phone, I noticed that Wynner had sent me a message. It slipped my mind that I had to call and invite her to the club tonight.

Hey, girl, what you up to? she said in her text message.

I'm heading to the club. Come out and chill with my sister and our friend.

I'm soo down. My husband been working so much, so I'm bored in the house. I'll be there in an hour or two.

Yass.

"Wynner is going to come out tonight. She's cool. Y'all going to like her." From the back, I could see Sundae scrunch her face up like she had an issue. "You got a problem, sis?"

"Damn, she pressed you," Tweeti instigated.

"No, I just hate when you try to invite all these new people around us."

"Invite new people around us? Sundae, who the fuck do I hang with besides my sister and you when you're not chasing another nigga?"

"I'm just saying. I don't want to be around a messy chick. Our circle is fine with us three."

"Bitch, be quiet because this is just a line. Your wishy-washy ass is always gone up some nigga's ass."

I wasn't surprised that Tweeti got in Sundae's ass. Wynner was nothing like the women that we despised. She stayed to herself and wasn't about anything messy. If anything, we could learn some shit from her.

"Fine. Y'all jumping down my back—damn." She decided to drop her shady-ass comment.

For the life of me, I didn't understand how she was pissed about someone being messy when her ass could be messy at times. For the remainder of the ride, it was silent until we pulled in front of the club.

"I gotta go in and change, so find parking. I'll see y'all at the bar."

When I walked into the club, my favorite bouncer wasn't working tonight. Winking at the one on duty, he allowed me through so I could go in the back to change. Usually, I never changed at the club because it meant I had to change in the back with the dancers. Today, I had a motive behind me going to change back there tonight. The club was packed with each section reserved. Dancers were doing private dances and jumping up on the pole.

Bottle girls were bringing buckets of liquor to the reserved sections. Everything going on tonight was telling
me that it was going to be a good night, and I was going
to go home with a bunch of tips.

Soon as I turned the corner to head to the dressing
room, Joey came out of his office with Kandle. He liked to
act like no one knew he was fucking a few of the strippers.
All those "talks" in the office weren't necessary. A few
times, he tried to have me come to the back to "talk."
Each time, I told him I was busy, and he could talk to me
right here.

"Remi, you just getting here?" he called as he slapped
Kandle's ass, and she giggled like the shit was cute.

"You so nasty," she cooed and continued walking out.

"What do you want? I'm not late, and I still have fifteen
minutes before I have to clock in."

He chuckled and walked closer to me. "I just was
saying hey. We're busy tonight, so I need you to close."

"Okay, am I being paid for the extra hours?"

He laughed once more like the shit was funny. I was
tired of him thinking that the extra tips I made were his
way of paying me. "Yeah, I got you."

"Let me go change and I'll be out there."

"Since when you change in the dressing room? You
always complain about the smell." He observed me
clutching my duffle bag.

"Well, maybe I would have changed, but I came straight
from work," I lied.

"Oh, okay. Hurry up because we need you out there."

Rushing down the hall, I turned into the dressing room
where the dancers were all talking shit, smoking, and
doing drugs to calm their nerves. Half of them went out
half-drunk every night to get rid of the nerves they had.
The smell in the room always smelled like sweat, sex, and
weed. Today, I was going in with a motive, and if I had to
smell this, then so be it.

"What you doing back here, girly?" Pop, one of the strippers, yelled to me. Smiling, I made my way to her station, where she was brushing her weave.

"Came from work. Just needed to change really quickly. You know Joey is always on my ass, so I couldn't afford to go home first."

"I admire you working so damn hard. Girl, I couldn't do it, and that's why I'm on this pole four times a week." She smacked her lips and sprayed some oil sheen on her weave.

"Let me ask you something, Pop."

"What's up? Don't tell me you trying to get up on the pole now."

Laughing, I shook my head no. It wasn't like I hadn't thought about it, though. "No, you know a nigga named Uzi that come by here?"

"The McKnight brothers? They're always here with their team or sometimes alone. Uzi messes with Kandle, though," she spilled the tea like I knew she would.

"They're together, or do they just fuck around?"

"She claims they're together, and he spends the night at her place; vice versa. I mean, when he comes in here, she's the only dancer allowed to dance on him and give him private dances in the back. We all know she ain't dancing in the back." She cackled and hit the table.

"What does he claim?"

"Uzi runs Harlem. Yeah, he has other boroughs that he makes money out of, but Harlem is his bread and butter. He's not about to go public and claim her ass. He may fuck, laugh, and whisper in her ear, but that's about it."

"So, he's a kingpin?"

"Uh-huh. Why you wanna know about Uzi anyway?" she questioned, side-eyeing me.

The best part of Pop was that she spilled everyone's tea. If you needed to know something, she was the one you went to. The worst thing about her was that you didn't want your business floating around the club. It didn't matter whose business it was. . . . She was spilling it if someone asked.

"Just asking. I saw him around the club a few times."

"Girl, who the hell you fooling? It's been a rumor around the club that y'all messing around. Now, are you gonna tell me, or am I going to have to pull it out of you?"

"We're not messing around. Me and Uzi are j—"

"What about you and Uzi?" Kandle's voice boomed through the room. This bitch thought she was Ronnie, but she was soon about to learn that I was Diamond.

"Damn, she heard her man's name down the hall," one of the other strippers joked. Kandle didn't think it was funny because she cut her eyes at the stripper who said it.

"I did. Why?"

Kandle acted as if everyone feared her in the club. The only person I feared was the man above, so this bitch could definitely catch these hands—and anything else that she might wanna catch.

"Well, Uzi is my nigga, and we've been fucking around for some time. I don't care what he told you because he gets around, and I'm constantly having to tell bitches who I am."

"Perhaps you shouldn't be with a man that is always around other chicks. If you're his woman, then you shouldn't have to keep reminding people."

"Remi, we don't speak, and I'd like to keep it that way. Just keep my man's name out of your mouth, and we won't have any issues," she called herself checking me.

"Sis, I'm not Nike, so you not about to check me. If I want to fuck with Uzi, I'll do what the fuck I please. Let me ask you this question. If you're so-called his chick, why the hell are you still stripping? I mean, this man has money, and you still shaking your ass on this pole, so what that say about your position in his life?"

Just as she was about to respond, Joey came into the dressing room and snapped his fingers. "I didn't know we paid y'all to have dressing-room confessionals. Let's get going and make this money, or I'll have some other bitches in here that will."

"You getting too slick with your mouth like I won't punch you in it," Pop voiced. Joey knew not to try her because Pop was the type to fight a nigga—and win.

"Pop, you know it's all love. Y'all wanna keep your jobs, right? With the owners making all these changes, I can't go to bat for y'all if you not working," he made some sad-ass excuse.

Kandle was the first to prance out of the room to do her set. I guess her money was more important than being dragged around this dressing room like a damn rag doll because if she kept the shit up, that's what she was going to get from me.

"You handled yourself well. Kandle is all talk," Pop whispered to me as I quickly changed into my uniform.

"I know how to handle myself, and I'm far from scared of Kandle's ass." With my answers in tow, I headed out of the back room and went behind the bar. Tweeti and Sundae already had drinks in front of them as they spoke among themselves. When they saw me, they waved me over.

"Bitch, you know we had to pay for these drinks. Joey's ass acting like he don't know who the hell I am."

"It's some new shit the owners are doing. I'm starting to think he's lying about the whole owner's shit. Anyway, I got y'all."

When I looked up, Uzi was coming through the door with Jah and two other men. Wynner was so short, I didn't even see her next to the man that I assumed was her husband. She was holding his hand and let go when she saw me. She was dressed in a denim miniskirt, white sheer bralette, and a nude pair of heels. Her hair was pin straight, and the makeup painted on her face was perfect.

"Babe, you damn sure didn't come to play," I smiled when she made it to the counter. "This is my sister, Tweeti, and our friend, Sundae," I introduced her to both Tweeti and Sundae. "And this is Wynner."

"Call me Wyn for short." She smiled and hugged the ladies. "I love your blond hair," she complimented Tweeti.

"Thank you, sugar," Tweeti replied.

Tweeti's eyes were across the club at Jah talking to some chick. They were smiling and kicking it. I could tell she was jealous because she kept rolling her eyes when they landed over on that part of the club. Uzi hadn't noticed me yet and was doing his thing.

"My husband, his cousin, and my brothers just had to pop out tonight."

"Shoot, the more people, the better. Let me go get these drink orders in and I'll come up to y'all's section," I promised.

"Come on, girls. Y'all can come up with us too," Wynner invited both Sundae and Tweeti.

While they headed up to their reserved section, I served a few drinks and chopped it up with a few locals. Lexi rushed over to the bar requesting her usual. Once she took down three shots, she sat on the bar stool and exhaled.

"Girl, these niggas are out here tonight. I'm out here trying to secure these bags, and I'm succeeding," she bragged, knowing damn well she wasn't.

"Three shots? Why?"

"Because I'm 'bout to do a threesome in the back with one of the other girls. You know I gotta be freakier than her so he can take me home instead."

"Need another drink?"

Trish nodded her head quickly and signaled with her hand to refill her cup. "Hell yeah. You coming to my crib tonight?"

"No, I came with my friend, so she'll drive me back home."

"Uh-huh. You think I haven't peeped Uzi coming around this club so frequently. You fucking Kandle's man."

"Kandle apparently don't got a damn man. A real man ain't 'bout to have his chick stripping in the club."

"How you know he's a real man, Rem?"

"I . . . I don't. I'm just saying." I slid her drink to her and watched as she gulped it down. "Be safe," I told her.

"You know I will. Make that money, babe," she told me and walked off to the back rooms.

After fixing a few more drinks, I finally left Trish to handle the bar. Everyone was over at the stages tossing money, so the bar wouldn't be too busy right now. Slipping away, I made my way upstairs to where everyone was. Tweeti was rolling her eyes, neck, and smacking her lips. Jah had another chick sitting on his lap, whispering sweet nothings in her ear. Wynner was sitting beside her husband nursing a drink, and Sundae and the other dude were smiling and chopping it up. Uzi had his face in his phone with a serious expression across his face.

"Remi, finally!" Wynner announced, and that's when Uzi put his phone down. He smiled when he laid eyes on me.

"Working girl finally got time for us?" he joked and came over to hug me. Ugh, his smell was everything. The Joop cologne that he was wearing had my senses in a frenzy.

"Hey. I had to handle business before coming up to check y'all. How you been?"

"I'm good. Just been doing the same shit you doing."

"And that is?"

"Securing these bags," he chuckled.

I sat down and crossed my legs. "Can't get mad at a man that's getting money. Besides all that, how have *you* been?"

"I'm good as fuck, now that you're here."

"Aw. Matter of fact, let me move away from you. Don't need your girl to run over here and get herself dragged."

"Who my girl?"

"Kandle."

He laughed and waved me off. "Man, stop jacking that shit. Kandle and me go way back. That's all."

"Is that so? Why she call herself pressing me in the dressing room over you?"

"Who?" Tweeti jumped up.

"One of his little girlfriends. I handled her; no worries, sis."

Tweeti sat back down and leaned back. "Get a fucking room!" she barked at Jah and his girl for the night.

"Why? I'm bothering you or some shit?"

"Nah. I'm just tired of seeing y'all all kissed up and shit. I'm trying to help shorty secure the bag. Sis, take the condom and run. He can't chase you."

Uzi choked on his drink and fell back on the couch, laughing hard. The nigga had tears in his eyes as he kept trying to stop laughing. "Yooooooooooo. This chick is my sis, for real." He laughed and stood up to sit next to Tweeti.

"If I'm sis, where the hell is my pair of Balenciaga sneakers?" Tweeti replied.

"I got you, I promise." He continued to laugh.

Even Jah laughed, but the girl didn't find the joke funny as the rest of us. "You've been eyeing us and rolling your fake contact eyes all night. You mad because you not on his lap, *sis?*"

"Those her real eyes, so you can stop hating now, baby."
No bitch was about to come at my sister. Her greenish
brown eyes are real, and everyone always assumed she
wore contacts. Like black people couldn't have colored
eyes.

"Did I ask you, though? Shouldn't you be downstairs
because they're taking a break?" She looked over the
banister. "Look like your coworker is having trouble
keeping up."

When I glanced downstairs, Trish was having trouble
refilling drinks before the next set of dancers came on.
Yes, I could have gone downstairs and ignored her, but
my pride wouldn't allow me to do it. Shorty called herself
trying to press me like I'm some punk-ass bitch and don't
handle chicks on the daily.

"You might wanna get down there too since you're so
thirsty to be down. Didn't I see you with another nigga a
couple of nights back?"

This chick was familiar, and the more I stared into
her face, I remembered where I knew her from. She was
always with different niggas and allowing them to buy
her drinks; then she heads out with them. Now, I don't
know if she goes to sleep with them, but after all those
drinks, I can't imagine they're going to her crib or his to
play Uno.

"What the hell is going on, Remi? Trish is down there
having a breakdown because she can't fill orders fast
enough, and you're up here having a good-ass time." Joey
came into the area with his arms folded like the true bitch
that he is.

"See . . . She down there struggling," shorty opened her
mouth to say.

"Get downstairs. What are you waiting on?" Joey
continued.

"Ask her nicely," Uzi demanded.

"This is her job. All I'm trying to do is my job, and that's what I'm doing. I joke around with you fellas, but I have a job that needs to be done."

"Nigga, ain't nobody joking when we say what the fuck we say. Apologize to her," Uzi stated again calmly. It wasn't a cool calm either. It was like the calm before the storm.

Joey was light-skinned and turned bright red. "You know what needs to be done," he told me and tried to leave, but Jah had pushed shorty off his lap and blocked the exit.

"You heard what the fuck he said to you. Ignore him, and I'll deal with you myself."

Taking a deep breath, he said, "Remi, I'm sorry for the way I acted. Please go down and help Trish out."

Laughing, I went downstairs and helped Trish out. Everyone was taken care of and back in their seats in under ten minutes. I headed to the back to get some more lime juice and ran into Joey.

"Finish up here. You're fired," he told me and handed me some money.

"*Excuse you?*"

"You're fired, Remi. I don't think I stuttered or said it in another language. Hand Trish the juice, and then you can leave. Please, don't make a scene because I don't have your last check. That money is for the extra hours you were *supposed* to stay."

For once, his ass was paying me for the hours I stayed, and I hadn't even done the hours. Then, he had the nerve to fire me and try to do it quietly because he was scared. "You can't be serious right now. I went up there when it was slow. Trish was supposed to call me when everyone came to refill their drinks. How are you firing me? I'm the best you have."

"I can find more or train Trish my damn self. Your mouth is crazy, and you feel like you can make your own rules."

"Man, I'm the best in the city. You think I give a fuck about this little shithole?" I screamed at him. "Fuck you, Joey."

With that, I went to the back to grab all my things. It pissed me off that because his manhood was tested, he wanted to blame me like I had done something personally to him. This job brought in good money and afforded me to pay my bills without struggling. My day job paid, but it wasn't enough to cover my bills without working overtime, which I hated. Pulling my purse over my shoulder, I headed back upstairs where everyone was. Tweeti could tell something was wrong as soon as she laid eyes on me.

"Are you all right?" Wynner questioned before my sister could.

Tears dripped down my face, and I sniffled.

"Yo, what the fuck that nigga did to you?" Uzi jumped up and held on to my arms.

"He fired me," I whimpered.

Now, I was a strong girl and could handle just about anything that came my way. Yet, when money was involved, I couldn't act tough. This was how I paid my bills and fed myself.

"Nah, I'm 'bout to go holla at him." Uzi took off, and I grabbed his arm.

"Please. Just leave it alone," I begged. "He has my last check, and I really need that money."

"So? I can pay you whatever that shit is," he continued, and I squeezed his arm even tighter.

"Please."

He saw my face and calmed down. "Yo, we heading out," he told everyone. Pulling my arm, we headed downstairs.

He didn't even give me the chance to say bye to anyone. Just as we were about to head out the door, someone snatched my damn arm—hard. "What the—?"

Turning around, I was face-to-face with Kandle. Her lipstick was smeared, which meant she was probably in the back sucking dick or some crazy shit. "Didn't I tell you about that one?" she said, pointing at Uzi, who was clearly annoyed.

"You warned me, and didn't I tell you about your so-called relationship? Right now, I don't need this shit."

Uzi pushed me to the back of him and stared down at Kandle. "Yo, why you doing the most? Chill the fuck out and go back to work."

"Uzi, you're such a man whore. Tell her how you were just fucking the shit outta me last week."

"Lira, I'll holla," he replied and continued to pull me out the door. He didn't use her stage name, which meant they *were* acquainted. This wasn't some random strip club hookup. They both had fucked around plenty of times to have been on a first-name basis.

When we got outside, Uzi held my hand as we walked to his car. It was parked right out front, and I wondered how he was able to swing that. This club didn't have valet services, and parking was scarce. He popped the locks, held the door open for me, and closed it behind me. I buckled my seat belt and sat there, still in shock that I had been fired. Joey was real fucked up to fire me over something that had nothing to do with me. His issues were with both Uzi and Jah, not me.

"He's a pussy nigga, and trust, I'm gonna deal with him," Uzi promised me.

"I don't need anyone's death on my conscience. He fired me, it's fucked, and I'll be just fine once I get over it."

"Nah."

"Nah?"

"Nothing." He was silent as we drove through Harlem.

Fifteen minutes later, we were pulling up to a tree-lined street with a bunch of those expensive-ass brownstones. His brownstone was the only one with a garage, which was different. It blended in well and didn't look out of place. Hitting the button on his visor, the garage doors opened, and he pulled beside one other car.

"Don't open that door," he told me.

I sat while he got out of the car, then came around the car to let me out of it. Getting out, I followed him up some stairs and into the kitchen. This kitchen was something right out of a home design magazine. The ivory cabinets matched the granite that had specks of ivory in them. All his appliances were stainless steel, which added to the ambiance of the room. Then, he had cookie jars lined up on the island with cookies all neatly piled in each jar.

"Stop standing around like you're a square. Sit down or something." He laughed to lighten the mood. Setting my duffle bag on the floor next to the island, I sat on one of the stools.

"Your kitchen is the bomb. You cook much?"

"Nah, my house manager handles all of that," he told me, like having a house manager was normal.

"Nice."

He went into the fridge to grab something to drink and nodded for me to follow him. When I bent down to grab my bag, he stopped me. "Leave that there. Ain't nobody 'bout to steal your shit."

Giggling, I followed him upstairs and down the hall to a room. He held the door open . . . and my mouth dropped at the huge room. In the center of the room was a king-sized, tufted, black velvet sleigh bed. Above the bed was an oil painting of this nigga with a rose in his mouth. I secretly pinched myself to see if I were dreaming, because this was unreal. Off to the side was a seating area with a TV mounted on the wall. His balcony had two French doors that led out to a balcony with two seats on it. Then, off to the side were a few closed doors.

"Wait, are you serious about this painting?"

"Hell yeah. I'm fired as fuck."

Shaking my head, I took a seat on one of the plush chairs in front of the TV. Uzi hit a button, and a wall turned around with a fully stocked minibar. It had everything from candy to liquor.

"Can I have something strong? I don't care what it is."

Nodding his head, he grabbed another cup and filled it with some Hennessy. Uzi handed me a glass, and I gulped it down quickly. He placed the bottle on the coffee table sitting between us. Taking the bottle, I poured more into the glass and took it back. The drinks started taking an immediate effect on me.

"Chill out. That ain't no regular Hennessy," he warned me. "This shit is aged like thirty years," he explained and sipped on it slowly. Everything he was saying was coming out slow to me . . . until I eventually blacked out.

Uzi

"Uh-huh. Just like I expected, she hasn't had any food and drank too much. Let her rest, and she'll be good in the morning. Well, not good, but she'll be alive," Clarise told me as she tightened her robe around her waist.

"You sure? I can take her to the doctor to make sure she's straight."

"Uzi, I've been around many drunk people and know what I'm talking about. In the morning, I'll put on some ginger tea with soup, because she'll need it," she warned me before she walked out of my bedroom.

When Remi passed the fuck out, the first person I called was Clarise. She came up and did her little mom shit and figured out that she had drunk entirely too much. When I told her how she only had two cups, she explained that she probably didn't have any food in her stomach prior to drinking the liquor I offered her. After moving her to the bed and having Clarise change her into a pair of my boxers and white shirt, she covered her up and told me what was wrong with her. A nigga was ready to call all the TV doctors, real doctors, and Olivia Pope to help me with this shit. Staring at my watch, it was three in the morning.

Walking into my bathroom with my cell phone, I dialed Lira's number and waited for her to answer. When it went to voicemail, I placed my phone on the sink and started to brush my teeth. As I was staring in the mirror at how fine of a nigga I am, my phone rang. Lira's name came across the screen. Sliding my finger across the screen, I hit the speaker button and continued to brush my teeth.

"Parrish, it's real fucked up that you flaunting that bitch around me at the club." She started off all wrong. I thought by leaving her ass in the club that she would get the message of coming at me correctly. Except, Lira never listened to shit and did what she wanted. She had been doing it since we were in high school, so I expected nothing different from her.

"You came touching shorty like y'all got some type of beef. Your beef with me, not her. Hell, your beef not even with me."

"We do. She call herself asking around about you. Wasn't I just at your crib and fucking you in the kitchen?"

"Word? She was asking about the kid?"

"Focus, Parrish!" she screamed. "Did you drop her home or something because I wanna come over?"

Lira probably done sucked hella dick, fucked mad niggas, and thought I was about to slide in there after that. I knew what she did and never complained because she was never my shorty. If she wanted to strip, then it was her free will to shake her ass all over the club for money. That didn't mean that I wasn't about to stop fucking her because she stripped. My jimmy was always strapped up when we fucked. Lira knew not to kiss me on the mouth or anywhere at all. It was standard fucking, nothing more or less.

"What the fuck you want, Lir? I like shorty, and I'm not 'bout to act like I'm not feeling her."

"Wow. One minute, we're supposed to be working toward something; then the next, you bringing another bitch in my face."

A nigga didn't mean to laugh so hard, but Lira was tripping if she thought we were ever "working toward something." "Fucking ain't working toward shit. I can fuck a turtle. Don't mean me and the turtle 'bout to be together forever. Go to bed."

"So, I can't come over?"

"Nah, I'm tired and got moves to make in the morning."

"Liar, but whatever," she accused me and hung up the phone.

Shrugging my shoulders, I took care of my nightly routine and showered before climbing in the bed beside shorty. Sports highlights were on, so I caught up on those while lying in bed comfortable as shit. Yeah, at times it was lonely going to bed in this big-ass shit by myself. Then again, I wasn't about to bring any bitch through my doors to fuck. Lira never made it past the damn stairs. If I allowed her to fuck in my room, then she thought she could come by and do it anytime. Every time she popped up unannounced, I knew she wanted to fuck, and I never hesitated to rip her clothes off . . . and then send her on her way.

I don't know when I fell asleep, but the sound of moaning caused me to open my eyes and turn to see if Remi was straight. She was tossing and turning and then jumped up in a cold sweat. By now, the sun had come up and the blinds I paid good money for to keep the sun out were doing a good job at keeping the sun out.

"Where . . . where . . . am I?" she stammered and touched her body. Her eyes scanned her body, and she gasped. "Oh man, oh man, oh man," she panicked.

"Rem, chill out. You're good."

She jumped when she turned and noticed me sitting up beside her. "Oh God . . . Did we fuck? I'm sorry, I do—"

"Chill, I didn't get to hit it yet. You drank too much and passed out last night."

Looking down at the shirt and boxers she wore, she stared at me. "Did you . . ."

"Nah. I had my house manager change you. You feel fine?"

She shook her head. "My head is pounding, stomach don't feel right, and I feel like I have to throw up."

"Chill out and lie back. Let me head downstairs and see where the soup and shit is." I got up and went to the bathroom to grab a waste basket. Shorty was fine as wine, yet she wasn't about to toss her cookies all over my bed and expect me to clean that shit up.

"I work today and can't miss work."

"You look like shit, and I'm saying that with all respect. I wouldn't feel right letting you go to work feeling and looking like this."

Sighing, she ran her hand through her hair in deep thought. "I appreciate that you care and all, but I have to work, or my bills won't be paid."

"I got you."

"No, I can't accept money from you. I have to get up and head to work. Do you mind driving me, or is that too much?"

I went into my closet and punched in my code to my safe. Quickly grabbing out a stack, I closed it back and came out of the closet. Remi was sitting on the edge of the bed, trying to get herself together. Tossing the money onto the bed, she stared at me, confused. If this was any other woman, she would have been grabbing the money and trying to push the whole stack in her bra. Remi stared at me and continued to try to get up. I knew it was hard, yet she was persistent.

"Take the money and handle your business. Worry about feeling better and not going to punch the clock for somebody else."

"I don't want your money." She moaned as she held her stomach. "Punching that clock affords me to live."

"And I'm telling you that you're not going to work today. Make that call and let them know that you won't be in to work this week."

"A week? I'm sure I'll be over this shit by the morning. You dragging it trying to make me stay out of work for an entire week."

Handing her the house phone, I left the room and went downstairs. When I got downstairs, Clarise was making breakfast and singing to herself. When she saw me, she smiled and pointed to the tray with all the hangover essentials that Remi would need for the day.

"She must be different, Uzi," she spoke without making eye contact. She was stirring the eggs in the pot.

"Something like that."

"I think it may be more than that. No woman has ever seen the inside of your bedroom. Especially Lira, and you've known her for forever. This woman is in your room, and you're catering to her."

"Clarise, you making it something that it's not."

She pursed her lips and rolled her eyes at me. "Am I? Take that girl the soup and tea . . . because your ass is sprung."

Laughing, I brought the stuff upstairs and placed it on the side table. Remi was in the bathroom throwing up. Knocking on the door, I peeked my head in. She was hugging the toilet and throwing up. My stomach felt queasy smelling the vomit in the air, yet I needed to hold her hair because it was all over her face.

"You good?" I said as I held my breath and tried not to throw up on her.

"Aaaaaargh." She continued to vomit into the toilet. It was like the smell was getting stronger and stronger.

"Nah, I'm 'bout to . . ."

I ran to the sink and threw up in the sink. Cleaning up bodily fluids wasn't my thing. I had a weak stomach when it came to shit like that. Like, I could kill a nigga and not blink, but if that nigga threw up, then I would be throwing the fuck up all over him before shooting him.

"Uz . . . Oh Lord, you *both* are sick now?" Clarise rushed into the bathroom to grab Remi's hair.

Wiping my mouth, I gagged and hurriedly stepped away from the sink. "You know all that shit makes me sick." I gagged and headed out of the room.

"Uzi, go into the bedroom and stay out of here. I don't need you fucking throwing up any damn more," Clarise scolded me.

Shit, she didn't have to tell me twice to leave. My body felt all queasy, so I sat down on the chair and stared at the TV. Clarise kept coming in and out of the bathroom with fresh linen, bleach, and a bunch of cleaning supplies. The last time she came out, she grabbed some fresh clothes from my drawers. A few minutes after, Remi came out of the room and sat on the edge of the bed. She had dark circles around her eyes, and the color from her face looked drained.

"Whatever liquor that was last night, you need to toss it the hell away. I've drunk on an empty stomach before, but this is on another level." She pulled the blanket back and lay down on my side.

"That bottle cost a few stacks. You lucky I allowed your ass to gulp it down like that."

She rolled her eyes and pulled the blanket over her body.

"All right, the bathroom is cleaned. You need to eat and drink that soup with the tea. Rest up, and you should be back to normal later tonight or tomorrow morning."

"Thank you soooo much," Remi smiled at her.

"No problem, pretty. We're bonded, 'cause I had to wash your damn body." Clarise winked, then headed out of the bedroom with the bleach and cleaning supplies.

"Damn, why didn't you call me to help?"

"Uzi, get your mind outta the gutta. This baby sick as hell, and you trying to get free grabs," Clarise laughed and headed out of the room.

"Ms. Clarise, he's keeping me hostage and won't let me go to work." Remi thought her ass was slick.

"Girl, the way you cut up in that bathroom, you might need to stay in the bed for the day. Drink and eat that soup with the tea," she warned again before closing the door.

"Damn snitch."

She giggled as I walked on the other side and climbed into the bed next to her. "You got my stomach all fucked up too."

"From the liquor?"

"Hell nah. I know how to sip my shit nice and slow. From you throwing up, *that* shit fucks up my stomach."

"How you a real nigga with a weak stomach?" she giggled as she sat up and started eating the soup.

"Ugh, this soup is gross."

"Who you telling? That shit has pulled a nigga outta a hangover quick, though. Clarise knows what she's doing."

"Is she your aunt or something?"

"Something like that."

"So, why is she cleaning your house?"

"'Cause she fucking stubborn and wants to, so I let her. Don't worry, human resources. I pay her very well."

"Okay, I'm just checking. I appreciate her helping me out and you worrying about me."

"It's all love, shorty." She smiled as she winced while eating the soup. "You need to call your man or something?"

"Here we go with this again." She rolled her eyes. "We're not together, and he wasn't my man, but he was my man."

"The fuck?"

"Yeah. It's confusing to me too. I'm still trying to figure out how I got roped into some shit like that."

"Shit, me too. He your nigga but not your nigga. You got my mental all the way fucked up with your situation."

Remi put the soup down and then grabbed the cup of tea. "We were never together; yet, he was the only nigga I was fucking at the time. He got hella baby mamas and shit. Still, he claimed he was out there claiming me." She rolled her eyes.

"You don't believe him?"

"No, because if he were claiming me, then he wouldn't have come over and let it slip that he has a daughter with his other baby mama on the way. Meanwhile, he got hella kids already."

"Shoot, you ready to be a stepmama? I mean, you could keep up with running around with them."

"Shut up, Uzi. . . . I'm not being no damn stepmama. I don't even have kids of my own, so I'll be damned if I'm gonna take care of *his* kids."

"On the real, you love the nigga?"

"No."

"You answered that too quickly."

"I know," she shot back. "We only fucked around, and that's it. If Shaq caught fee—"

"Shaq? From New Brighton?"

"Yes."

"Nah, you fucking that nigga?" I cracked up laughing. She didn't find it funny from the expression on her face. "Yo, he tries so hard to be put on. Nigga been asking around about who to speak to, and my niggas that sell out there haven't said shit."

"His weed is trash."

"Reason why I'm not 'bout to put him on. If a nigga could still push trash weed, then he's a nigga that will do what he gotta do for money."

A real nigga wouldn't be wasting their time on trash weed. In fact, they would go to the person who sold the shit to them. Here he was, selling fucked-up weed and trying to act like the shit was normal, and he had the loud. Nah, nigga, you got the quiet, as in you need to sit in the corner and be quiet.

"Aw, put my man on for me, please." The look I gave her made her sip her tea and be quiet.

"Don't play with me."

She looked confused. "What?"

"Don't act like that nigga is your man. You said he's not your man, right?"

"Yeah."

"So, that nigga ain't your man."

Remi put the teacup on the side table and got comfortable under the covers. "You jealous?"

"Nah, why would I be jealous about something that's already mine?"

This shit got serious when she brought Shaq into this shit. He was some small fish; yet, if he knew that I wanted Remi, he wouldn't hesitate to get in her ear to have something that I wanted. The nigga was asking around about who he should speak to when he knew he had to come to me. Remi was rough around the edges, and that's what I liked. She didn't let you tell her anything and go with it. Shorty had a mind of her own, and judging from the stack of money lying in the same spot, she wasn't about the money either.

"Correct me if I'm wrong, but you just said that you can't be jealous of something that's yours?"

"No need to correct you. You right."

She started blushing and shit, so I moved closer to her. "This tea got me all hot and stuff." She pulled the covers off, and I stared at all the tattoos on her body. Shorty didn't just have a few here and there. Nah, her entire body was marked up. The only place that didn't have a tattoo was her face. I was all for tattoos and had some myself, but, damn, she put me to shame with her body art.

"All these tattoos are dope as shit. What made you mark your body up like this?" When I asked the question, I noticed she shut down. All the smiling she was doing as my finger outlined the heart on her thigh stopped.

"They're just tattoos," she vaguely answered.

She should have known that I wasn't about to let this go without her speaking on it. Seeing her reaction piqued my interest. "I ain't stupid. I know what they are. Fuck made you do it?"

"Drop the subject, Uzi, please."

"Nah, somebody was beating on you or something?" That was the only logical reason why she would cover her entire body, then act the way she did when I asked about it.

"Huh? What? No." She snapped out of her daze. Sitting up, I stared at her until she was forced to stare into my eyes. "Since I asked about your tattoos, you been acting wild weird."

"Why are you all in my business? If it's not something I want to talk about, why you keep pushing it?"

"Tell me why the fuck you acting all crazy and shit." She climbed out of the bed and held on to the side table to catch her balance.

"I'm better off going to work than sitting here with this shit."

"Then maybe you should."

"I will." She walked into the bathroom and slammed the door.

This wasn't how I expected this shit to happen. All I wanted to know is why the fuck she was acting all stupid and shit. She could have an attitude all she wanted, but her ass wasn't leaving this crib until she felt better.

"You could have all that attitude right now, but when I come back from getting me some soda, your ass better have that shit fixed."

"Fuck you, Uzi."

"Only if you want . . . be naked then." With that, I left the room and went downstairs. Clarise was showing out, 'cause her ass never got started on dinner this early. She had everything chopped and ready.

"Why you up there screaming at that girl?" She watched me as I grabbed a bottle of soda.

"She acting like a fucking weirdo and shit."

"How?" When I explained what had just happened to Clarise, she shook her head at me. "Maybe she doesn't want to share it with you. Did you think about *that*?"

"Yeah, and I don't care if she doesn't wanna share the shit. She *gonna* share the shit with me. I'm risking a lot having her in my crib and knowing where I lay my head."

"What makes Remi knowing where you live different than Lira?"

"Lira will always protect me for obvious reasons." I held my dick in my hand. Clarise shook her head again and put the seasoning on the chicken.

"And another unspeakable reason?" she added.

"You starting to sound like my mama now."

"Yes, and when are you going to answer her calls? She called here a few days ago asking if you've been home."

"I'll check in with her sometime today or tomorrow."

"She just wants the best for you, Uzi."

"So I've been told." I headed out of the kitchen and went back upstairs. When I walked into the room, Remi was putting her shoes back on.

"Look, I don't want to argue with you. I'm not going to work, but I am going the hell home," she copped the plea soon as she saw me enter the room.

"Nah."

She stared at me, confused. "Nah?"

"You heard what I said. I'm feeling you, and each time we've kicked it, you confirm the shit more and more for me. This the one time we can kick it and our lives aren't interfering with the shit. So, nah, I'm not about to let you leave. I mean, if you wanna leave, that's your choice. I'm not 'bout to hold a chick hostage if she really wanna go." She stood up and headed toward the door. "Act like you don't know me when you see me though," I added that last part.

As I stared out the window, I could see her reflection in it. She hadn't walked out of the bedroom and was just standing there. It was as if she were going back and forth about what to do and trying to decipher what I meant. Remi quickly turned around and lost her balance in the process.

"You have some nerve saying that I need to act like I don't know you. Why? Because I don't want to share something personal with you?"

"Yep."

"How can you be so nonchalant? So, all that talk you've been doing was bullshit? You can act like you don't know me?"

"Yeah. You see who the fuck I am. I can't afford to let people get close and end up hurt again. . . ." My voice trailed off before I got too deep into my own shit.

Remi walked a few steps closer to me. "Then, I guess this is goodbye." She turned around and walked out of my room.

Like hell. I wanted to go after her, but I knew that nothing would change. She wouldn't tell me what I needed to know, and I would end up questioning everything about shorty. When I walked over to the bed, the stack of money was still lying there. At least she didn't want me for my bread, I guess. That could be the positive out of this shitty situation.

Wynner

Last night was perfect, and it felt nice to spend time out with my husband. It had been so long since Qua and I had gone out and just hung out. At first, I was sad about us putting baby making on hold, but now it felt like it was the best thing to do. Yeah, he was gone a lot more now because Uzi had given him more responsibility, but when he did come home, we didn't talk about babies and the things I needed to do to check if I were fertile. It was us just talking about regular stuff and laughing. I still hoped that we would welcome a baby into this world sooner than later, but I couldn't be so focused on having a baby that I neglected my husband and his needs.

After Uzi and Remi left the club, Lira had found me and cried on my shoulder. How was I supposed to tell her that she didn't have anything to cry about? Uzi and she would never be together, and I think everyone that knew them knew that. Lira was only something for Uzi to do when he was bored. Remi was someone that I could see him with. From the few times that we hung out together, she was sweet, smart, and had just the right amount of sassiness that would keep Uzi in his place. The problem with Lira is that she was too clingy and wanted to always be under him. After she finished crying, some man pulled her to the side, and that was the last I saw of her for the rest of the night.

While Qua, Grizz, and Jah spoke business over drinks, the girls and I continued to drink and turn up. Tweeti and Sundae were both really cool. We had a few drinks, and then I left Qua to get breakfast with them from IHOP. It felt nice hanging with a group of women that didn't want to hang with you simply because of who your brother was. Tweeti was very outspoken, which was new to me. I was the complete opposite when it came to being vocal. For as long as I could remember, I was always Uzi and Jah's younger, quiet sister. The only time I really expressed myself was when something had been building and I couldn't hold it in anymore. That's when I had to take a step back and let everyone know how I was feeling.

"You good, babe?" Qua asked as I finished my breakfast at the island. I didn't want to tell him, but I could feel a flare coming on.

There was no rhyme or reason to why a flare started. I just knew the symptoms and knew that meant I needed to calm down and take time for myself. Although Qua asked me the question, his head was down into his little phone. It seemed like since he had been back from Miami, something changed. He was gone more, and I knew it was work related, yet he didn't bother to call me anymore. It irritated me that I was feeling like I was only getting a piece of him lately.

"Yes, I'm fine. Just tired from last night. Why are you all dressed?"

He placed both his phones and wallet in his pockets and shoved my medicine closer to me. "Gotta handle business. What are you doing for the day?"

"Hoping that I could spend it with you. I see that's no longer an option."

Qua walked around the island and spun me around in the chair so that I faced him. Then, with his right hand, he lifted my chin up and looked down into my eyes. "Babe, you know that I need to work. All of this shit here isn't free, and Uzi really came through for a nigga. It's about getting this money so I can get out."

"How has he stepped up? You're not telling me a lot of things, and I can tell." He tried to stare off to the side, but I grabbed his chin and forced him to stare into my eyes. Qua couldn't and wouldn't lie to me, so I knew he was about to spill what he had been keeping a secret.

"Uzi handed me Brooklyn. I'm in charge of everything that has to do with Brooklyn," he revealed—and the pit of my stomach sank.

I knew what I signed up for when I married Quamere. There was no doubt that he was going to get into the game to make our lives better. My life was already provided for, but he wanted to be able to give me the same things I was accustomed to, which I explained wasn't necessary. This game didn't have loyalty, and everyone was out for themselves. To hear that he was in charge of Brooklyn scared me. I was fine when he was doing things here and there for Uzi . . . but taking over a whole borough was a different story.

"I don't want to be burying you, Quamere." Tears slid down my cheeks as I studied his face.

Wiping my tears with both his hands, he pulled my head closer to him, then kissed me. "Aye, what did I tell you about thinking like that?"

"It's hard *not* to think like that. You're out of the house more than you are in."

"Yeah, I know. . . . Look, I gotta make a few more trips down to Miami to handle some things. Once all this work is done and settled, I wanna take us somewhere romantic. Just you and me."

"That's all nice, but I'll believe it when I'm getting on the plane." My lips were poked out, and my eyes were rolled in my head.

"Oh yeah. . . . You'll believe it when you see it?" Qua tickled me and caused me to snort with laughter. He knew I hated to be tickled.

"Okay, okay. I believe you." If I didn't give in, I would be pissy from him tickling me too much.

"Finish your breakfast and get out of the house. There aren't too many days that you feel good enough to get out." If he really knew how I was feeling, then he'd demand that I stay in bed.

I was determined not to let lupus get me down. Today, I planned to hang out and have a good day, even if I was alone. After kissing Qua and walking him to the door, I plopped down on the couch and dialed Remi's number. The phone rang a few times before it went to voicemail. I dialed again and was greeted with her voicemail again. Since she left with Uzi last night, I dialed his number and, like always, he answered on the first ring.

"Baby girl, what it is?" he coughed after he greeted me.

"Is Remi still with you?"

"Yeah, she sleeping. Last night, she had a few too many drinks and is paying for that shit now."

"Oh."

"Everything good?"

"Uh-huh. Just was going to do some shopping and hanging out."

"Call Tweeti. Y'all kicked it last night and seemed to be on the same page. Rem is gone to the world right now. Just listen." He put the phone to her, and all I heard was snoring.

"Dang. All right, I'll call them. Talk to you later."

Before I could end the call, Uzi said, "Wyn?"

"Yeah."

"Everything good with you?" he asked again.

"Uh-huh. I'm just hanging in there. You know me."

He chuckled and then allowed me to end the call. Before dialing Tweeti's number, I washed the breakfast dishes, then straightened up the kitchen. Qua loved to cook breakfast . . . until it came to cleaning up the mess he almost always created. Once I was finished, I climbed into bed to relax for a bit before dialing Tweeti's number. Her phone rang a few times before her groggy voice came through the line.

"Dang, you still asleep?"

"Was. Before your ass called. What's up? I'm up now."

"If you need to wake up, I'll call back."

"Nah, I'm up already. Should have been up, but I'm up for real now. . . . Jah, move the hell over," she added before yawning in the phone.

"Wait! Jah's there?"

"Uh-huh. He came knocking on my door an hour after I got home. Guess homegirl wasn't it for you, huh? I mean, since you claimed you were into bigger women." It was like I wasn't on the phone anymore. Her conversation had shifted to one with Jah.

"First off, you not about to wake me up with some bullshit, Tweeti. Leave me the fuck alone and give me blankets!" he barked at her, and she grew silent.

"One sec, girl," she told me.

"Ooouuuch, why the fuck you push me onto the floor?" Jah yelled.

With me being on the phone, they were so loud that it felt like I was in the room with them. "Next time you call yourself being slick with me in my damn house, you gonna get slapped *before* being pushed on the floor," she warned.

"Umm, I can call back."

"Girl, don't worry about that. Anyway, what you doing today?"

"I wanted to check if you girls wanted to grab lunch and do some shopping."

The line grew quiet.

"I'm down. Just need to make sure everything is cool with Remi. She didn't come home last night."

"I called Uzi, and he said she's sick from drinking too much last night. So, we can head to his house after lunch and shopping."

"Sounds like a plan. But, uuuh . . ." Her voice trailed off.

"What?"

"We don't have a car, so where you wanna meet. Sundae had to take it back this morning."

"That's fine. I'll come scoop y'all up. What time should I come get you both?"

"Come around twelve. I'm gonna go shower now and be ready."

"Nah, she 'bout to get this dick first, sis. Call back in two hours."

My stomach turned hearing my brother say those words. I knew they both got pussy and were offered pussy on a daily basis, but that was something I would rather not have any part of knowing.

"You not sliding into this, Jah. Keep playing with me."

"Damn, so you kicking me out when you leave? I'm tired as fuck."

"No, you can stay. I know my snacks better not be all gone, though," she warned him before we confirmed plans once more and ended the call.

It took me no time to shower and head out to Tweeti's place. The traffic wasn't too bad, so I made it there in record time. The only thing I hated about living in the city and owning a car was traffic. Sometimes, it took me over an hour to travel just a few blocks. Uzi and Qua both agreed that I couldn't catch a cab unless I was with either of them. It was annoying to have overly protective brothers; then to turn around and have a husband that acted the same was a headache. My body was killing me, and I knew I should have kept myself in the house. A day of shopping and hanging with Tweeti and Sundae sounded so much better. Remi's number popped up on my car's screen. Pressing the green button, it connected the call.

"Your brother is really warped," was the first thing I heard before I could greet her on the phone.

"What happened?"

"He broke up with me because I wouldn't share something personal with him. Shit, we weren't even together for us to break up. So, why the fuck does it feel like a breakup? Damn, I'm tired of getting with these niggas that ain't my nigga," she vented all to herself.

"Relax. It will all blow over soon, and you guys will be cool."

"Nope, he said to act like I don't know him, so that's exactly what I'll do," she tried to convince herself.

"You like him, don't you?"

"Doesn't matter. He's not going to act like I'm not important. If he could just cut me off now, what happens when we're more serious?"

"Where are you now?"

"In the half bathroom in his kitchen," she replied.

"Girl, what? You didn't even leave the house?"

Even she had to laugh. We shared a laugh together as I gained access to the expressway.

"Yes, he had me so pissed that I had to get out of there."

"Do you want me to head over there to pick you up?"

"No, Clarise told me I can stay downstairs in her guest room. I feel like crap, and this headache feels like there are children playing the drums."

"Oh yes, you need to lie down and get some rest. Don't worry about anything because Clarise will have you."

"Thanks. You need to speak to your crazy-ass brother," she giggled. "Like, he was so serious that it hurt my feelings."

"It's his way or the highway. Remi, if you are serious about my brother, that's something that you have to take under consideration. Parrish likes things his way or no way at all, and if you guys get serious, then that's something you have to deal with."

The line grew quiet.

"It's something that I would have to think about. Everyone can change, so he'll have to change his ways with me."

"You can try, and I wish you all the luck if you could get him to change, but he's usually stuck in his ways. I've tried for years to get him to change his views. But, hey, you can always teach an old dog new tricks."

"Right now, I'm willing to turn some tricks to get this headache to stop."

"Remi!" I cracked up laughing.

"What? If you felt this headache, you would be out there with me."

"Tell Clarise to give you some medicine out of the cabinet in the downstairs bathroom. I'm on my way to Staten Island to hang with Tweeti and Sundae."

"Yass, I'm glad that you guys hit it off last night. Tell Tweeti I'm sleeping because I can't hear her loud ass right now."

"Yeah, thanks for introducing them to me."

"No problem, you're one us now," she giggled. "Have fun, and call me later," she told me.

"Okay, feel better."

Once we ended the call, I drove all the way to Staten Island without traffic. When I went past the toll plaza with the cashless tolls, I knew I was near. Following my GPS, it wasn't too long before I pulled in front of a building.

Outside.

We're coming, Tweeti replied back.

"We're coming" usually means that you're actually coming downstairs. Tweeti and Sundae didn't come down until twenty minutes later. Popping the locks, they got into the car and were staring at me.

"Who the fuck shows up to the project in a pink matte Audi?" Tweeti laughed as she reached over and hugged me.

"I didn't feel like finding the keys for one of Qua's cars."

"Did this bitch say 'cars'?" Sundae yelled from the back. "Bitch, we don't even have one, and your ass got options."

"Y'all crazy. Where do y'all wanna hit first?"

"First off, your damn brother is crazy. He doesn't wanna leave my house with his crazy ass." Tweeti blushed when she mentioned Jah. There was something there, and she was acting like there wasn't.

"Jah is the sanest one."

"Humph. So, how crazy are the rest of y'all's asses?" She looked around like someone was watching her.

"What are you looking at?"

"To see if some more siblings may pop out of the bushes on me."

"Girl . . ." we laughed.

"Let's grab some food. I'm starving."

"Sounds good with me. I had breakfast, but I'll get something small."

"*I'll get something small,*" Tweeti mocked me. "You didn't get thick from watching your weight," she added.

Little did she know, it was food and the steroid medicine I took for my lupus. When I had flares, that was what helped stop them as much as they could. They didn't work all the time, but when they did, it was a semigood day.

"Anyway, I saw you and Grizz, Sundae." Both Sundae and Grizz hit it off last night. They were in their own little corner, minding their own business while the rest of us hung out.

"We sure did. He's a big-ass man, but I can handle all of that," she confidently announced. "Size aside, he's really cool and has a different outlook on things."

"He told you about his past?"

"Nope, and I don't wanna hear it until he tells me himself."

"Dope. I like that you want to hear everything from him. Never listen to another woman tell you about your man, although I've been knowing him long, and he's like a big cousin to me."

"Nothing personal, but I've listened to women tell me about a man, and then I get crazy." She looked away. "I'd rather have him tell me what's going on and deal with it when he tells me."

"Understandable."

"Now, what is going on with you and Jah?"

Tweeti tried to look out the window and act all shy. "Why you all in grown folks' business?"

"Girl, we're the same damn age," I called her out. "Tell me what got your head open about my brother. I mean, I know Jah's dope, but I wanna hear it from your mouth."

We decided on Perkins down the street from their house. It was a small franchised diner, so I knew they should have some good food. There weren't too many, if any, of these in the city. The hostess sat us down and handed us menus.

"Tweeti, spill."

"You *are* persistent, just like your damn brother," she laughed. "I like him, dammit. He's different, and I don't say that because he's in a wheelchair. I've only counted a few people to keep it real with me. In the short time we've been talking, he has proven to be added to that list. He's always so real about everything, and he doesn't sugarcoat anything. Then, that smile of his has me gone." She messed with her hair as she spoke about him.

Even though Jah called himself overly protective of me, I was just as much protective of him. Women like to skip over the fact that he's a human with feelings. Some of them see a money bag sitting in a wheelchair and think this is their way out of the hood. So, when he started talking to women, I was leery of even getting close to them. Tweeti didn't seem that way at all. Jah knew when someone wanted him for his money, so the fact that he continued to chase her proved that she was a good person.

"Aweee, I could tell he likes you too. Jah hasn't smiled like this in forever. He's so happy and open about how he feels about you."

"Well, he needs to be open about how he feels about me *to* me. All I know is that he likes to sleep over at my house, and I'm gonna need him to tell me. Then, what was with that chick from last night? That's one of the things that makes me pause in my tracks."

"Don't worry about her."

"Wynner, I'm *gonna* worry about that. I don't take too kindly to getting my feelings hurt, so I need to know."

"And I'm telling you not to worry about it. I know my brothers, and if he feels how you do, you won't ever have to worry about another chick."

"I'm gonna trust your ass *for now,* but let a small piece of my heart get hurt, I'm kicking ass."

"I promise."

We ended up ordering the same thing. As we waited, Tweeti decided to dig into my business. It was nice sharing girl time and getting to know these girls, but I wasn't ready to spill what I had been going through. Especially since my own family, besides Jah, didn't know.

"You married real young. What was the rush? Daddy made you get a shotgun wedding?" She shot each question off, one after another.

"My dad didn't even know I was getting married. We ran to city hall and got it done."

"Really? I would have thought y'all would have had this nice elaborate wedding," Sundae commented.

"Nope. I mean, he has always asked if I wanted to renew our vows with a huge wedding, but I told him no. What's the need? That day we got married was special to me, and I don't need to try to replace it with a nicer wedding."

"True. And the bitches that spend all that money on a ring and wedding be the ones crying because they nigga fucking the maid or butler."

"*Butler?*"

"Yep, shit happens, and you gotta question these niggas. Do he like pussy or wanna get his booty tickled."

"Amen, because if a nigga come to me and tell me some shit about him being gay, I'm gonna go to jail." Sundae waved her butter knife.

"Don't get me wrong, I love my gay men and have no problem with them being gay. Shit, life too short to not do what you want. What I don't accept is the men that are married and taking it up the ass on the low. If you're gay, you need to leave your woman and find yourself alone. Don't drag a whole woman down with you."

"Go ahead and preach, Tweet." Sundae clapped her hands loudly. The patrons of the restaurant, the majority of whom were white, were staring at us.

"I agree. All that big wedding stuff isn't important to me. My mom wants me to have one because my dad was robbed of walking me down the aisle, but it's not important to me."

"Even if you don't have a big one, let your dad walk you down the aisle. Every father dreams of doing that. It's not about you; it's about your father. We know you're fine with how you and Qua married. You do have to think of your family and what you robbed them of, though," Tweeti replied.

Not once did I think about my father and my family when we went to get married. To me, what was done was done. They couldn't take it back, and there was no need to speak about it. Listening to what Tweeti said, it made sense why my mother still talked about it. She loved and admired Qua, yet she was sad about how we decided to get married.

"Your mama was robbed to help plan a wedding with her daughter. You know, all those cute, fun things you do when you plan a wedding."

"You're right."

"Now, I'm not saying go and have a big-ass wedding because of us. Just give your parents something to hold on to."

"I hear you."

"You're the baby," Tweeti added.

"And the only girl," Sundae commented. "Anyway, I need that food to come because I'm starving." She rubbed her stomach.

I loved my parents more than life. Thinking back, I made this about myself and never thought of my mother. She had only me. I was the only girl, and she had dreamed about planning a wedding for me, and then I went and tied the knot myself. I practically robbed her of being able to show me off to her friends. We've gone to plenty of weddings for her friends' kids, and she always told me mine would be better. Growing up, I didn't think she was serious, and as I got older, I didn't think about her. When Qua asked me to marry him, I thought about my family and cried. It wasn't that I was robbing them of the chance to celebrate my special day. I was more worried about what they would say, and more, about how my brothers would react.

Mama, we need to talk, I sent my mother a message.

Everything all right?

Yes, just need to talk to you.

Okay, we can do lunch this week, doll. I love you.

Love you more.

We received our food and decided on our next plans. I knew I had to tell Qua, and he wouldn't care, because he told me to do it years ago. Right now, I was trying to ignore the burning I felt in my body and focus on hanging with the girls. It wasn't every day that I got to hang out and have girl time. It felt nice, so lupus was going to have to take the backseat today.

Qua

They said God doesn't give you more than you can bear, right? Well, the way I had been out here working to secure this bag proved that to be true. When Uzi told me to take out the men that ran Brooklyn before I came in, I was skeptical. Then, when I spoke with those dudes, I knew for a fact that they were stealing bread and trying to pull a fast one over. Grizz and I put our black Tims on with our hoodies and handled that shit. It was quick and easy, and I made it home to climb in bed with my baby. If Wynner knew what I had to do to take over shit for Brooklyn, she probably wouldn't sleep at night. I hated lying to her, but this was the best thing for her. The less she knew, the better off she was.

Since taking over Brooklyn, the streets required my undivided attention more and more. Of course, I would have loved to kick it with my baby and spend the day together, but money needed to be made. This morning, I needed to have a meeting with my team, and that took me away for three hours. Wynner hit me a few times, and I had no choice except to send her to voicemail. Rather than walk in the crib empty-handed, I decided to take a quick trip to the Gucci store and surprise her with that python bag she had been hinting about. She would appreciate the fact that I came here in the first place since she knew I couldn't stand shopping in these stuffy-ass stores.

"Quamere Classon?" I heard my name being called. Since I stayed low and didn't involve myself in shit in the streets that wasn't my business, I wasn't paranoid. Whoever it was had to have known me to know my full name.

Turning around, I was met with a thick caramel woman with a pair of jeans that looked as if they were painted on. Her brown, doe-shaped eyes blinked as her white smile captured my interest. Shorty's hair was pulled into a thick ponytail that hung down her back.

"Who wants to know?"

"You really don't recognize me?" She acted shocked.

"Shorty, I see a lot of faces in the day. You expect me to remember you?"

Laughing, she cut her eyes and then flashed a bright smile. "Yo, Olay!" She mocked a man's voice, and I stopped in my tracks.

"Olay muthafuckin' Vega? Where the fuck is the braces, glasses, and terrible-ass skin?" I seriously asked as I went and embraced her. "Damn, you were just up and down. Where'd these curves come from?"

"Turns out eating fried chicken and all that soul food gets a sister right," she giggled. "How are you, Quamere? It's been forever," she smiled.

I felt like this shit was a blast from the past. Olay had always been that cool chick that you chilled with and considered one of the homies. She had these thick-ass glasses, braces, and was like a hundred pounds soaking wet. Yeah, she wore tight shit, and everyone just overlooked her and considered her a homie. Olay ended up moving to Cali because her moms got a job out there. The night before she left, she asked me to take her virginity. I would be a fool to say that I didn't think Olay had a crush on me. The way she would stare at me and shit, I knew she was feeling me. I ignored her because I didn't see her like that. This was before Wynner, and I was focused on just trying to survive day by day.

That night before she left, I dicked shorty down something serious. When she left my room at the group home, she was walking all types of funny. We kept in touch for a few months; then the communication stopped. Shit, I had other shit to deal with and didn't have time to wonder why she stopped reaching out. Now, seeing her standing in front of me, I could tell time had been good to her. Those braces worked wonders on those shiny white teeth she had up in her mouth.

"Damn, I'm good. What you doing back in New York?"

She messed with the tips of her hair. "I came for business and decided to stay a day extra to shop and kick it with my family. That purse looks good on you." She pointed to the purse I held in my hand.

"Stop fucking playing with me," I laughed. "You still in Cali? I mean, tell me what's going on with you?"

"My mama is still in Cali. I moved to Miami to pursue modeling," she explained. I didn't know what type of modeling she was doing because she wasn't tall at all. "So, now I model and do a few videos and stuff. Nothing major." She shrugged her shoulders.

"That's lit. You gotta let me take you out to dinner or something before you leave. We gotta catch up."

She sighed. "My flight leaves tonight. . . . I wish I would have run into you earlier." She sucked her teeth.

"I'll be in Miami next week, so we'll def link."

"Oh, yeah? Is this trip already planned, or do you feel the need to come to Miami since seeing me?"

I laughed because she was dead serious. "Nah, I got business to handle down there. But, we'll link when I come down there."

Hugging once more, we exchanged numbers and shit; then she left the store with her two shopping bags. "Sir, I have the bag at the register. Whenever you're ready," the saleslady said, touching my shoulder gently.

"Appreciate it," I said and continued looking around. My baby deserved the entire store, so I was going to do my best to buy the shit out.

As I was looking at these latex sock heels that I knew Wynner would kill for, Grizz walked into the store. This nigga had been outside waiting because he hated stores like this, just as much as me.

"Damn, the fuck taking so long?" His loud voice caused the salespeople to jump out of their skin. All of them were behind the register damn near huddled together. This big six-foot-seven nigga, who weighed over three hundred pounds, would scare anyone.

"Chill the fuck out. My wife need some new shit, and I'm gonna bless her with some."

"Oh, that shit got nothing to do with Olay fine ass walking out of the store, huh?" he commented.

Grizz knew Olay from back in the hood too. We weren't real cousins, but being that we were both failed as children, we made our own family. Nobody could tell us that we weren't related by blood. Before he got locked up, he tried to shoot his shot with Olay. This nigga called it when he said she would be a baddie when we were older.

"How the fuck you recognize her? She walked up on me, and I didn't know who the fuck she was."

"Nigga, I follow her ass on Instagram. Shorty pretty big on there."

"Damn. She had to have her body done or some shit. I can't see Olive Oyl Olay, man."

Grizz let this hearty-ass laugh out that even startled my ass. "Shit, I don't know. You done in here? We need to head to Staten Island to pick up Jah."

"Staten Island? Why the hell that nigga in Staten Island?"

"Tweeti. He spent the night at her crib last night."

Shaking my head, I asked the same girl for Wynner's size and went to the front to pay for all this shit. "What's good with you and shorty?"

"Who, Sundae?"

"Yeah. Y'all was all in the corner, chatting it up and shit." The older lady behind the counter frowned at my use of language as I handed her my credit card.

"She cool as fuck. I'm supposed to be linking with her tonight over some drinks and food."

"Word? Make that a double situation and both Wyn and I will slide through."

"Nah, I need time to get to know shorty. Take your wife out on your own time," he chuckled as we left the store.

"Fuck you, nigga. I'm gonna take her to Nobu. You know how she feel about that place."

"I don't. Shit too expensive there."

"Cheap ass. Here." I tossed him the keys as I put the bags in the trunk.

All things told me that I shouldn't have been thinking about Olay as we drove to Staten Island. I mean, I was married and happy, so it shouldn't matter that I ran into an old friend. Then again, shit ended with us and never was explained. Why did she stop calling me? We lost contact, and at the time, I didn't give a shit. Now, I was sitting here, wanting to know the reason for the dropped communication. Wynner was my world, and I would never do shit that could jeopardize our union. My baby stayed down with me when I didn't have a pot to piss in or a window to throw it out of. In the end, she was my real one and proved to be. She could have left and been with a nigga that was getting more bread than me. Because she didn't, I would forever spoil her and make sure she was straight.

"Word? Bet. I'll swing by there before coming to scoop you." I listened to Grizz talk on the phone. His voice got all soft and shit, so I knew he was talking to a chick.

When he ended the call, I laughed because this nigga tried to act like he wasn't just sweet-talking and shit. Picture this big-ass nigga on the phone sweet-talking a female. The shit was hilarious.

"Shut the fuck up. Shorty asked me if I could pick her up some eyelash glue."

"Nigga, *what?* Y'all ain't even together, and she got you picking shit up? Next, she gonna have you grabbing pads and shit."

"Oh, like how Wynner got you doing? Stop trying to play me like your wife don't got your ass wrapped around her small-ass fingers."

It wasn't like he was lying. Wynner could have everything she wanted and more when it came to me. I just dropped over eight stacks on a pair of heels and purse for her. The thing that made me want to spoil her was that she never expected, nor asked for, the shit. It was because she didn't expect the shit to be done, and it was the reason I did all I did for her. Wynner didn't grow up like I did. I mean, her pops had a name in the streets, so they had a little bit of money. When he blew up was when they moved, and she was pampered like a princess. The shit that turned me on about Wynner was that she could have acted entitled, turned her nose up at me when I approached, and a bunch of other shit.

Instead, she smiled and spoke with me, then handed me her cell number. It was a bunch of shit that could have gone wrong the day I approached her on the block. There were many times when she had to help me out with bread and did it without any problems. When I asked her to marry me, I didn't have a ring or a plan. All I knew was that I needed to grind to continue to provide for my future wife and our future together. Even with her being constantly sick, she was still the most beautiful woman in the world to me. At times, she cried because she felt like I was there for her more than she was for me. I never paid attention to any of that shit because she was my world, and I did all I did because she deserved that . . . and more.

"Damn, that toll is expensive as fuck. Who the fuck over here? Obama?" Grizz complained.

"Shit, if he over here, then we need to convince him to come back to the office. Forty-five fucking the world up."

"Dead ass," Grizz agreed as we drove through the cashless tolls.

It didn't take us long to arrive at the address that Jah sent us. When we pulled up to the projects and saw Jah on the phone barking on somebody, we knew we were in the right place. I jumped out and allowed him to do his thing. Once he was in the car, I grabbed his chair and put it in the back.

"Nigga, I'll rip your fucking tongue out of your mouth . . . fuck with me!" he barked before hanging up and tossing his phone in the seat beside him. "Fuck is up, pussies?" he laughed, then dapped both me and Grizz.

"Same shit, different day," Grizz replied. "How you, man?"

"Shit, I'm chillllllllliiiiing," he laughed while clapping his hands.

Even I had to turn around and stare at this nigga for a minute. Since shit went down with Jah, he wasn't as he was now. He joked here and there and smiled, but that was it. He stayed to himself and didn't bother with anybody. Hearing this nigga in the back, spreading all this joy, had me a little tickled. Did this have to do with Tweeti? He damn sure came out of her building and was now all happy-go-lucky and shit.

"Nigga, you on dust?" Grizz asked.

"Nah, just loving life right now," he replied. "Tweet got my nose open like a cokehead in a damn coke party."

"The fuck? Nah, you definitely doing dust."

He punched my arm and laughed. "Shut the fuck up. Like, on the real, I can't explain the shit. She got me feeling all good and shit."

"She let you hit?"

"Nah, that's what got me all confused and shit. I ain't even thinking about hitting, though. All I wanna do is be near her."

"Oh, so now you feeling how I felt about your sister. At least she don't have two cockblocking-ass brothers."

Jah laughed hella loud, and Grizz turned back around again. "Nigga, if you don't shut your loud ass up with all that laughing, I'm 'bout to put his ass on the sidewalk."

"Wynner is baby girl, so niggas had to cock-block. Even now, we still on her because she's the princess."

"I feel you; I feel you."

We pulled away from the curb and headed back into the city. Jah needed to go bark at one of his workers out in the Bronx. Me and Grizz didn't have shit else to do, so we decided to drive around with him while he handled his business.

Grizz dropped me off at the crib from running around all day. Jah had us driving his crippled ass all around until we eventually dropped him off at his crib. The nigga went home, grabbed some clothes, and then was on his way back to her crib. Shit, she argued about him snoring and his bitch from last night. Still, she agreed for him to come back over there. I meant to ask him what the fuck they had going on because he was just with the next chick the night before, and now he was talking about how much he was feeling her. It didn't matter what was going on; I liked that he was getting back to himself.

When I walked into the crib, Wynner was sitting on the couch with Chinese food. She turned around and smiled when she saw me walk into the living room with two bags. Chewing on a piece of chicken, she eyed the bags with wide eyes. Her ass knew these bags were for her. Wynner did all my shopping because I couldn't stand shopping. Yet, for my girl, I would be in the stores like a damn shopaholic.

"Look at your ass, drooling at the mouth and shit," I joked, and she rolled her eyes at me.

"Stop it. I'm not drooling," she giggled. "When did you go to Gucci? Lemme see, lemme see." She clapped her hands while bouncing on the couch.

Setting the bags in front of her feet, she didn't hesitate to rip through them and open each box. "Baby, I love these. Thank you so much." She rushed into my arms, causing me to fall back onto the couch.

"Damn, what I get for doing so good?"

Winking, she stood up and unbuttoned the silk shirt she had on. She slowly unbuttoned each button, then stopped when a perfect view of her lace bra started to peek through. "You gonna have to come and find out," she winked and pranced off to the bedroom.

Grabbing the box of opened Chinese food, I took a spoonful for energy because I was about to break her back with the dick I was gonna hand her. When I got into the room, Wynner was leaned on our bed with her arms folded with this cute-ass smirk on her face. Her jeans were unbuttoned, and she had pulled those down just enough so I could see the matching lace panties. Damn, she wasn't playing fair at all, and she knew it.

"You missed this dick, didn't you?"

Nodding her head, she bit down on the side of her lip with lust written in her eyes. "Very much, daddy," she cooed.

Walking over to her, I tugged her jeans down to her ankles and ripped open her shirt. I'm sure this shirt cost me some bread, but I didn't care as the buttons flew to the floor. Pushing her onto the bed, I pulled the rest of her jeans off and then spread her legs. The lace on her underwear allowed me to see her pussy just smiling at me. My wife's body had me in awe each time she was naked or even fully clothed. She was thick in all the right places. Wynner's ass was stacked, and her thighs were thick as hell. When it came to her waist, it was nonexistent, and her flat stomach had a little pudge to it, only because she loved to eat.

"I want it hard," Wynner moaned as I pulled at my pants to give her what she wanted. My dick was busting through my pants and drawers as I rushed to unhook the belt and drop the shit on the floor.

Pulling my shirt off, I tossed it to the side and climbed between her legs. "I ain't even taking the panties off," I growled as I bent down and sucked on her neck. Marking my territory was something I loved to do.

Wynner complained because she had to walk around with dark-ass hickies on her neck all day. Shit, that just meant that niggas knew that she was taken, if they decided to ignore the rock on her ring finger.

"Baby, I gotta talk to you about something," she moaned as I continued to suck on her neck.

"Oh yeah? About what?"

"I . . . I want to have a wedding," she moaned.

"Yeah, we can do that."

"Babe, I'm being serious."

I kissed her neck once more and leaned up to stare at her. "Wyn, you serious?"

"Yes, I was doing some thinking, and the girls had brought something to my attention. What we did back then, we thought about ourselves and not about our family."

"Shit, I don't have no family except Grizz, Wynner. Being that he was locked up, there was no other family to think about."

"Baby, my parents didn't get the chance to see me get married. I wanna do this for them, and, of course, us. We don't have wedding pictures anyway."

"The hell you talking about? We got one right there."

She rolled her eyes when I pointed to the printed picture of us in front of city hall that day.

"Professional ones." She rolled her eyes.

"We can do this. You know I would marry you over a million times. . . . Let's do this." She smiled when I gave her the stamp of approval that she knew I would give. "Ma, you hate doing wedding stuff, so who gonna do it?"

"My mama will plan the entire thing. I don't want anything to do with it, except showing up."

"Word, me too." I started kissing back on her neck. She lay back on the bed and rubbed my back as I spread her legs, and my dick fought to find its favorite place to hide.

"Thank you, baby."

Between kisses, I stared into her eyes and winked. "You wanna marry a nigga all over again. You so in love," I teased her.

"Shush and give me what I've been asking for." She wrapped her legs around me and pushed me into her tightness. Wynner was the only woman that this shit felt right with. The way I fit so perfectly inside of her drove me crazy.

The way she moaned quietly and stared directly in my eyes as I gave her these deep strokes drove me crazy. It was as if she were telling me that she trusted me and that every part of her was mine. Anybody could tell you those exact words, but it meant more when you could read them in someone's eyes. Wynner was my baby, and I couldn't leave her even if I tried. During our marriage, we dealt with her hospital stays, miscarriages, and the hate Uzi showed our marriage; yet, we made it through. She never backtracked and sided with her family once. Even when shit got rough, I told her we could annul the marriage and remain friends. Wynner slapped the shit out of me, walked out of my homie's crib, and didn't speak to me for days. Imagine how crazy I was going knowing my wife was out there in the world and wasn't speaking to me. The shit ate me up and made me realize how those words I told her were easy to say but hard to do.

Wynner's legs wrapped tighter around my legs, and she kissed me on the lips. She bit my bottom lip as I dug deeper and deeper into her. Heavy breathing and soft moans were all that could be heard in the bedroom. We had a rough couple of months, so having this moment where I was making love to my wife without all the extra shit attached felt like everything.

"Oooh, right there," she gasped as her head dropped back, and she allowed me to bend her legs upward.

She did gymnastics all during junior high school, so imagine how flexible she was in the bedroom. "I love you, baby," I said through clenched teeth as I continued to pound her insides.

"Love you too, baby," she replied and threw that pussy at me. Looking at the clock, I smirked because we were about to be at this shit all night. I finally felt like I was getting my wife back. When God saw fit, we would be blessed with a baby that we would love and raise together. Right now, it wasn't our time, and we needed to enjoy ourselves and life before a baby came into the picture. Tonight is exactly what I planned on doing.

Remi

Uzi had me all types of fucked up when he told me that I better not speak to him again. Half of me was ready to walk out the door and go home. The logical side told me to go downstairs and calm down. I wasn't feeling the best, and the ride back to Staten Island from Harlem would be a long one. I still couldn't believe that Joey's pussy ass ended up firing me. That money was something I needed in order to take care of myself. I could always pick up more hours at the hospital, but they were always stingy when it came to who could work extra hours. It was funny how when they needed me, I could work. Then, when *I* needed the extra hours, they had to approve it and make sure I was "able to do it." Thinking about work and losing my job just made me feel worse than I already did.

Clarise offered for me to stay in her guest room. I declined and ended up camping out on the couch with plenty of snacks, soup, and tea. She even brought me down a nice heated blanket, along with the remote and password to the Netflix. Uzi hadn't come down once since I had settled in here over eight hours ago. Clarise finished her work for the day and told me that she cooked stewed chicken, rice, peas, and plantains. After, she said, she was taking her son out for the night and would see me in the morning. I liked that woman, and the fact that she didn't hold her tongue made me like her more. She was so comfortable that I assumed she had to be related to Uzi in some way.

Switching the channel, I settled on watching *90 Day Fiancé*. The love-and-hate relationship I had with this show drove me nuts. One second, I couldn't stand how stupid Jorge was when it came to Anfisa. Then I couldn't take my eyes off the screen and not watch. This was my all-time favorite show and caused me to be extra leery of men, with the way Mohamed did his wife, Danielle. Tweeti hated when I watched because I would scream at the TV and scare the shit out of her. Grabbing my phone, I dialed my sister's number and waited for her to answer.

"Yas, aw shit, right there, Jah," she moaned into the phone.

"Seriously? Get it in then," I cheered her on.

"Girl, quit. I'm kidding. How you feeling? Wynner told me how you were feeling."

Laughing, I started choking and stopped. "You're so stupid . . . and is that him in the background making sounds too?"

"Yeah, he stupid. It was his idea." She broke out laughing. The two of them were laughing hard as hell while I held the phone away from my ear.

"Y'all done?"

"Yeah, but what you doing?"

"In the living room watching *90 Day Fiancé*."

"The living room? Where's Uzi?" she questioned.

"Upstairs. We got into an argument, and I told him I was leaving. He doesn't know I'm down here."

"Girl, go up there and speak to him. How you in a man's house and not speaking to him?" Tweeti asked as if I cared. *He* was the one that came at me left. I was cool down here minding my own business.

"Nope. I'm fine right here."

"Well, how did the argument start?"

"He asked about my tattoos."

Tweeti sucked her teeth. "You always get so weird when it comes to your tattoos, Rem. We're close as hell, and *I* don't even know why you decided to dedicate three years of your life to marking your body up."

"Because it's my business, and nobody needs to know."

"I'm not going there with you again. We're about to watch *Bates Motel,* so call me later when you stop being stubborn."

"Will do. Later," I told her and ended the call. Placing my phone on silent, I lay back on the couch and got engrossed in this show.

It was rare that I had time to rest my body and just chill. If I were home, it was only to change clothes before switching jobs. This wasn't home, but it felt damn near close because I was comfortable as hell. Mentally, I was prepping myself to have a conversation with Tweeti about Jah. They seemed to be spending a lot of time together, and I wanted to know what was up with them. They were cute together, but I didn't want her to hurt that man.

"Fuck you still doing here?" Uzi poked his head into the living room. Why the fuck was he so rude, and why didn't this man put clothes on? He had on a pair of white boxers and a Versace robe that he had opened.

"I wasn't feeling well enough to travel, so Clarise told me to stay down here. Don't worry, I'll be out your hair in the morning."

"Bet." He left the living room, and I lay back down.

Here I was, minding my own business when this nigga came back with a bowl of chips. Sitting on the opposite side of the sectional, he tossed some chips into his mouth and started to smack loud as hell. It was clear that he wanted to tap-dance on my nerves. He wasn't going to get a rise out of me today because I wasn't in the mood to argue with him for the second time. Turning the TV up a little bit, I continued to pay attention to the show.

"Weak-ass show," he scoffed.

"Uzi, would you like to watch TV? I could have sworn that you have a damn eighty-inch in your bedroom."

"Don't matter. All these shits in this crib are mine."

"Wow. You always fall for the dickheads," I mumbled to myself as I turned on my side to continue watching the show.

"So, you fell for me?" He *would* have good-ass ears. Just my damn luck that he would hear what I mumbled under my breath.

"I like you, yes." There was no need to act like I didn't. Uzi was cool to be around, and the way he tried to cater to me, although he had a weak stomach, was sweet of him.

"Like you too," he grumbled. All I could do is laugh because his ass was so damn childish. Here he was, sitting there being a big-ass baby for nothing.

"So, why do all of this? We could have been hanging out the entire day."

"Tell me about your tattoos," he continued with this shit again. This time, he looked at me with sincere eyes. He was staring deep into my eyes, and I felt comfortable telling him.

"I . . . I just don't want to go to that place."

He set his bowl on the coffee table and scooted over, near me. "Ma, I'm not asking you to tell me for my health. I wanna know about you, on the real. Yeah, I could have left the situation alone early when you started acting weird about the shit. Check it, I like you and wanna know what you like and dislike." He touched my thigh and stared at me.

Taking a deep breath, I looked away, but he guided my face back toward his. "When I was 17, I was raped. My mother had a card game going, and one of her friends found his way in my room. I was doing my homework and minding my business. Tweeti was at a sleepover at her friend's house. He wasn't drunk, high, or anything," I paused. Uzi moved closer and pulled me into his arms. His embrace was warm and made me feel so comfortable.

"He closed the door behind him, then locked it. The music was so loud that when I was screaming, no one heard me. This man was about two hundred pounds. I fought the best I could until he slammed me on my neck, picked me up, and had hi-had his way with me." My words started to break up. The lump in my throat formed as I tried to keep the tears at bay.

"Damn, that shit just pisses me the fuck off." Uzi tightly gripped his own knee. Placing my hand over his, I stared into his eyes.

Sniffling, I continued. "It didn't matter how many times I showered and tried to scrub my skin, I never felt clean. When I walked outside, I felt like everyone could see the rape on my skin. It sounds silly, but that's really how I felt. Imagine holding on to your virginity while all your friends handed theirs up . . . only to get it robbed from you. There was no sense in telling my mama because she was so consumed with fighting her own devils. How could I burden her with some more issues?"

"She's your fucking mother, Remi. Her job was supposed to be to protect you, and she failed."

"It wasn't her fault," I defended. "When I was old enough, I started getting tattoos. There was something about the pain that made me addicted to them. The more I got, the more I felt like they were a disguise, hiding the pain I carried on my skin. They were something beautiful to look at, yet kept me protected at the same time. It sounds dumb, but it's the feelings that I've felt for years."

He pulled me onto his lap and held my chin. "Tell me the man's name," he demanded.

"He's dead. Died from liver cancer a few years back. Guess his Karma came to collect," I let out a small chuckle.

"That should have never happened to you, Rem. I'm sorry if I made you open up some emotions you weren't ready to reveal right away, but I'm happy you felt comfortable enough to tell me."

"All I ask is that you never mention this to Tweeti. To this day, she has no clue that happened to me, and I'd like to keep it that way."

"What I look like going around telling your business? I mean, that's some personal shit, and I don't run my mouth. I'm not no fucking bitch." He took offense and made me giggle.

"I trust you won't say anything, Uzi."

"Can I say something now?"

"Yeah."

"When I was 18—" As he was about to speak, his phone started ringing in his robe pocket. He grabbed the phone out of his pocket and placed it to his ear.

"What?" He pressed the button for speakerphone. I guess from me sharing a bit about myself, he felt comfortable talking business in front of me.

"Yo, your sister is in the hospital. We've been here an hour. She woke up sweating and couldn't catch her breath," Qua's voice came through the line.

"Another flare-up?"

"Seems like it, but I wasn't trying to take any chances. When she said she couldn't breathe, I got her over here quick as fuck," he explained.

"Bet. I'll be there in a little bit. Hold it down."

"Always," he replied, and they ended the call.

Uzi ran his hand down his face and sat there for a second before he dialed Jah's number. When they finished talking, he stared at me for a bit.

"Is Wynner all right?"

"She will be."

"You answered your phone in front of me on speaker. You trust to speak business in front of me?"

"I ain't never gonna speak business in front of you. Don't matter if I trust you or not. A woman's place shouldn't be involved in my line of work," he voiced to me.

"Oh."

"You could be my wife, and I won't speak business in front of you. It's not because I don't trust you. It's because I don't trust people. The less you know, the better."

"I understand."

"Get your sexy ass up so I can head to the hospital." He tapped me on the ass, and I slid over.

"How is Jah getting to the hospital?"

"Grizz is going to pick him and Tweeti up," he explained.

"I'm coming, then."

"Go put some clothes on," he told me.

We both went upstairs, and I found a pair of sweats of his, a T-shirt, and True Religion hoodie. I slipped my feet into my sneakers and was ready. Uzi was dressed similar to me as we headed out. It was raining, so he held the umbrella for me, then opened the door before getting in on his side. His parents did a very good job of raising him. I felt so classy with him holding umbrellas and doors for me as if I were a celebrity. Uzi was quiet as we drove to the hospital. I placed my hand on his knee and offered him a comforting smile. It was crazy how we both went from arguing and being done, to being the comfort for each other. I've never spoken about my rape to anyone. For years, I've held it in and battled it alone. For once, it felt nice to tell my side of what happened. I didn't have a voice for so many years, and now it felt like I did. The man was dead, and I couldn't bring him back, but knowing that he was six feet in the ground helped me sleep a little easier at night.

"I want you to be my girl," he randomly said.

Beyoncé's *Lemonade* album was playing on the radio, the raindrops were hitting the top of his coupe, and the gray clouds were visible, even in the night sky. Those were all the things I noticed while trying to control the butterflies in my stomach.

He didn't repeat himself or get an attitude because I didn't answer. Instead, he turned the radio up, and we continued to drive as his hand rested on top of mine. I reached for the knob and turned the music down.

"Okay."

He was silent and then turned to stare at me quickly. He smiled and then turned his attention back to the street. "Bet."

"That bar shit is dead. Don't go look for another job at another bar. All that tight shit you were wearing for those niggas is a dub being with me, you hear?"

"That's how I make money, Uzi."

"If I gotta pay all your damn bills, then I'll handle it. You not going back to that club shit." He was stern when he said that. For now, I was going to leave the situation alone. Wynner's words were in the back of my head. There had to be a compromise in a relationship, and being that we just got into one, we needed to establish that early on.

We arrived at the hospital and entered holding each other's hand. The front desk let us know where Wynner's room was. I wondered what was wrong with her and if she were fine. We had just spoken earlier, and she sounded fine. Hearing that she was in the hospital had me worried about her. I wanted to make sure that she was fine and everything was good with her. I allowed Uzi to go into the room first. This was his baby sister, and they needed their time together. Qua came out of the room and smiled.

"How you?" He gave me a quick hug.

"I'm good. Is Wyn good?"

"Yeah." He sighed, but he didn't sound convincing. "I'm 'bout to run down to the vending machine to get her favorite cookies. Tell Uzi I'll be back."

"All right."

Outside her room was a small waiting area for visiting families. I sat down, crossed my legs, and started to read on the Kindle app on my phone. My attention was all into *Shorty Fell In Love With A Dope Boy*. This book was bringing me through my emotions. As I was about to flip the page and find out what the hell Church was up to, Tweeti stood in front of me.

"Is she all right?" she asked as she took a seat beside me.

"I don't know. I didn't go inside. Uzi went inside so they can have their family time, you know?"

"Yeah. Babe, go inside the room and see what's up," Tweeti told Jah. He nodded and rolled into the room.

"Umm, *excuse* you? *Babe?*"

Tweeti laughed. "I call everyone babe. We're not together or even spoke about it. We're just chilling and hanging out. No relationships over here."

"Does *he* know that?"

"I don't know. We haven't spoken about it, and no, we haven't fucked yet. Dick still work and is big," she felt the need to mention.

"Ugh. Why do you have to mention that? You think I wanna hear about your boo's dick?"

"You wanna be in my business about everything else." She rolled her eyes. "We're hanging out and taking it slow. I like him, Rem. Just not trying to get hurt again, you know?"

"Yeah, I hear you."

The door opened with both Uzi and Jah coming out. "Y'all can go in," Jah told us.

Both Tweeti and I held hands as we walked into her room. When we walked inside, we expected her to be on ventilators and stuff. Wynner was sitting up in the bed on her cell phone, scrolling Facebook.

"Hey, girls." She smiled weakly. I did notice she didn't have as much energy as she usually did. Her voice was low, and the lights were low.

"Hey, boo, what happened?" Tweeti came around the bed and hugged her. "Are you all right? I need to fuck Qua up?"

Wynner laughed and shook her head. "I have lupus," she revealed.

I've heard about the disease and had a few family members that had the same thing. I heard it was a very hard disease to live with. Being that Wynner was around Tweeti's and my age, it was so sad that she had to battle this so young.

"Wow. I would have never guessed."

"I usually don't like to tell people because they start to feel bad for me. There are good and bad days, so those days I don't wanna come out with you guys, just know it's because I can't."

"Then, we'll come to you," Tweeti took the words right out of my mouth. "We don't like too many people, but we clicked with you. And it's not because of your brothers, either. If we were done with them tomorrow, I would still be calling to hang with you."

"Thank you, y'all. It makes me feel better knowing that you guys care." She smiled.

"What are the doctors saying?"

"I'm having a flare-up. This time, my breathing was shallow, and I felt like I couldn't breathe at all. They're keeping me for a few days to see if it returns."

"Good. I'll be up here until you head home," I told her.

"Okay, okay okay. Enough about me. What's going on with you and Uzi?" Wynner giggled. She knew what was up and just wanted to hear it from my mouth.

"Yeah, what's up with y'all? Shit, *I* wanna know."

"We're dating."

"How'd that happen from arguing?" Tweeti asked.

Shrugging my shoulders, I said, "We just talked, and he asked me on the way here. I told him, okay, so we're together. Gag is, he doesn't want me to apply to any other bar jobs."

"His way or the highway," Wynner chanted. "How do you feel about that?"

"I'm upset. That's how I make my money, and I've been reaching out to other club owners, and they want to hire me. We're too new of a relationship for him to pay my bills. We'll be burnt out and tired before we make it to a year."

"Everything that you just told us, you need to tell him the same thing," Tweeti spoke up. "You can't give up the life you had before him. Hell, he met you at your bar gig, so he doesn't have to like it, but he has to respect it at least."

"Yeah."

"Can I be honest with you two?"

"This bitch! I thought we were friends." Tweeti rolled her neck. "One thing that I'm not, I'm not fake, and if you keep it real with me, then I'll do the same."

"I don't feel woman enough for Qua," Wynner confessed.

"Huh?" She had me confused by what she said. Wynner was more than woman enough for Qua. She was woman enough for *any* man, so she had me confused.

"Before I woke up and couldn't breathe, Qua and I were getting it in. Like, we were really getting it in until we fell asleep. That's when I woke up and felt like I had been run over by a train, which is normal when I have a flare-up. I knew one was coming on, but still went shopping with you and Sundae," she explained. "But when we were driving, he mentioned that he wasn't going to be rough anymore like we had been hours before. Told me I'm delicate and blamed himself. If my husband can't get his sexual frustrations out on his wife, he'll go find someone else," she sobbed.

Tweeti took one side, and I took the other, and we hugged her. "Babe, he loves you, and from what you tell us, he's not going anywhere. It doesn't mean he'll cheat. It just means you guys will find other ways to have your time together," Tweeti said as she hugged her tightly.

"You have to understand that as your husband, he was probably scared out of his mind. You're his wife and world, so it's normal for him to blame the sex part of it on the reason you couldn't breathe and felt like your body was hit by a truck," I then told her.

"Maybe," she replied, not convinced at all. This wasn't something that just popped into her head. She had to be feeling like this for a while.

"Wyn, just talk to him about it. Don't hold it in, please," I begged her. From experience, I knew that holding stuff in is never healthy.

"I will." From the way she answered, I could tell she was lying to me. This was her marriage, and how she decided to deal with it was her business. Friends always seemed to cross that line and try to tell someone how their marriage should be. The only two people that should be concerned with their marriage were the two people that were actually in it.

We stayed around and hung with Wynner until around five in the morning. Jah told Tweeti he was taking her home because he had to handle business. Uzi had pulled Qua to the side after a phone call, and Qua didn't look pleased. After saying our goodbyes, I was on my way back to Uzi's house to climb in bed to sleep. He told me he had to do something and just dropped me off. Clarise let me in, and I went straight to his bed and went to sleep. Being the girlfriend of a kingpin was tiring.

Tweeti

"You miss me?" Jah asked me as we sat on the phone. My mother was having her weekly spades card game, which she said she wouldn't anymore, but here she was hosting another one.

"That depends."

"On?"

"When I'm gonna come over to your house. You've been over here, and I've never been to where you live."

If Jah wasn't home, he was here. The only reason he didn't come over tonight was that I told him I was going out. When the plans fell through with Sundae, and she ditched me to hang with Grizz, I ended up calling him to talk on the phone. It was ten at night, and although he was a grown-ass man, I didn't want him coming out this late. Don't get me wrong, I didn't doubt that he could protect me and himself. It just didn't make sense for him to come all the way here when I didn't want to be here.

"Damn, why the fuck is it so loud?"

"Evelyn is having her card game." I rolled my eyes in my head as I listened to her loud and drunken-ass friends.

"What I told you about calling her that?"

"And what did I tell you?"

"Come over," he told me.

"Seriously? 'Cause I really don't want to be here right now," I whined. Remi had gone from work straight to Uzi's house.

They had been spending a lot of time together lately. Wynner was still in the hospital because of blood clots in her legs. If it wasn't one thing, it was another. Earlier, I spent a few hours with her, and she was ready to come home. It had been two weeks since she was first admitted to the hospital. As her friend, I tried to keep her spirits up and continued to visit so that she could keep herself sane. Each time she told me her mother or father were coming to visit, I left. Jah's parents were off-limits, and I didn't want to meet them right now. We weren't together, so there was no need for me to meet his parents at this time.

"I'm sending a car service to get you now," he told me. Smiling, I stood up and started gathering some clothes and stuff I needed.

"How long am I staying? Because I need to know how much to pack."

"However long you wanna stay. I been at your crib more than here, so feel free to do the same."

"And you been getting on my damn nerves."

"Yeah, whatever. He'll call you when he's downstairs with the car," he told me as I grabbed a few things from my closet.

"All right."

As I was putting clothes into my bag, my mother opened my door. "We're loud. I'm not gonna have you coming out there acting like I don't pay bills in here too—straight embarrassing me," she spoke her broken-ass English.

"I'm leaving, Evelyn. Be as loud as you need to be."

"Where's your sister?"

"At her boyfriend's house."

"Boyfriend?" She raised her voice, shocked.

This is what happened when you weren't involved in your children's lives. We were grown and didn't need her to take care of us anymore. We still needed her to be there as a mother and give us advice. Once in a blue moon, she came wanting to talk and catch up on our lives. It was a sad situation, so I avoided opening up to her. For what? So my heart could get broken when she was concerned about herself and getting high?

"Yes, she has a boyfriend. You need to speak to her about that because I'm not telling her business."

"Tweet-Tweet, where you going?"

"To a friend's house."

Eventually, she got the hint that I wasn't about to tell her anything and left. My life was private when it came to my mama. A few things I shared with Remi and she'd happen to be there and would find out things about my life. As for me voluntarily sitting down and spilling my business, it wouldn't happen with us. If my mother decided to get her life together, then we could work on having a relationship, except she wasn't, and when we spoke about it, she shut us out about it. Even if we didn't have the best relationship, I prayed daily for her.

Just as I finished putting my earrings on, I received a call from the driver. He stated he was downstairs and ready whenever I was. Usually, when I called a cab, they were screaming how they would pull off if I wasn't downstairs in three minutes. So, this was different to me. Luckily, I was ready to get the hell out of here and head to Jah's house. My mama was in the middle of a game when I headed out. She didn't even see me leave, but I knew I had to lock my bedroom door. Not that she would steal my shit. I didn't trust the people she ran around with, and if something of mine was missing, I wasn't going to remember that they were my elders when I beat their ass.

A Lincoln Navigator was waiting downstairs. The driver got out and held the door for me. Once I was inside, I grabbed a complimentary bottle of water. The driver got in and smiled at me through the rearview mirror.

"Good evening. How are you doing, ma'am? Is it too warm in here for you?"

Being that October was coming in, the weather had been warm as hell. Usually, I would be able to wear a coat, but the weather wouldn't permit it. At nights, it was cold as hell, and since we lived near a beach, it was colder here than anywhere else.

"It's perfect. It got cold out there."

"Tell me about it," he chuckled and pulled off.

Jah never told me where he lived, and I never asked. I figured he still lived with his parents since he couldn't walk and would need help. When we crossed the bridge going into Jersey, I was shocked that he was actually that close to me. We drove another thirty minutes before we pulled up to a modern house. It was so nice and modern that I thought we were at the wrong address. It was gray concrete with stone columns. The garage doors were glass, and you could see a Porsche in the garage. The landscape had these beautifully trimmed hedges out front with rock incorporated into the landscaping. There were three other houses in the area that were fairly close to each other.

"Well, we're at Mr. McKnight's residence. I think you're the only person I've brought here besides his family," he informed me.

"Why is that? I don't want to go in there and find out he's a damn crippled killer."

He let out the loudest, heartiest laugh. "No, he's just a very private person. Let me grab the door for you," he told me and got out.

Grabbing my bag, I climbed out of the truck and walked up to the front door. Even the front door was see-through, and I could see his foyer. Ringing his doorbell, I laughed because only he would have a doorbell with a camera. My heart skipped a beat when I saw him roll to the front door and open it.

In Love with the King of Harlem   219

"Welcome to mi casa." He held his arms open, and I reached down to hug him. Jah's nasty ass gripped my ass, but I ignored it.

"Well, this is how the other half lives. And why do you like to stay at *my* apartment when you have all of *this?*"

"Because you're there," he admitted, then rolled down the hallway.

My ass was blushing like crazy as I followed behind him. He pressed a button, and the elevator opened. We stepped inside and were brought to another floor. When the elevator door opened, the view of the city right across the water was like a huge oil painting. On his balcony, he literally had a beautiful view of New York. There was a huge TV mounted over a stone fireplace. He had the fire going, and I was so consumed with this house he had that I didn't notice that I smelled food. The whole kitchen, living room, and dining area were an open floor plan. Each part of the room had a beautiful view of the cityscape.

"This is beautiful, Jah. Like, I would never leave if I lived here."

He rolled into the kitchen and grabbed a bowl. "I ordered some food and shit."

Looking at the table, this man had flowers on the table and candles lit with a bottle of champagne. "Oh, did you? It looks like somebody was trying to impress Tweeti."

"Nah, you not about to talk about yourself in the third person. I was having dinner and just added a plate so you can eat too."

"Seriously? You were having a fancy-ass dinner like this alone? You fronting so hard, but I'll let you live. Where can I put my bag?"

"I gotta treat myself good, right? My bedroom is the last room down the hall," he pointed.

"Uh-huh. Somebody feeling the kid." Walking down the hall, I found his bedroom. You would think a man in a wheelchair would have different changes to his home to help make his life easier. Instead, everything was regular and unmodified.

Digging through my bag, I found some pajamas and went into his bathroom. The bathroom was the size of my current bedroom. His shower had about three damn showerheads and was all glass. In his linen closet, I found some towels and washcloths. It didn't take me long to get undressed and hop in that shower. Since I didn't bring body wash, I used his and spent a little while bathing. The water felt like everything pouring all over my body at this moment.

Once I was done, I put on my pajamas and went into the kitchen. Jah was on the phone, so I sat at the kitchen table. The food was set, and I knew it was probably cool. Nobody told my ass to go shower when I was supposed to place my bags down. When he finished, he came to the table and stared at me.

"Shower was good?"

"Yep."

"The view was even better," he admitted.

"Pervert. This looks good. Where'd you order it from?"

"Some Chinese spot I order from a few times."

We served our food and started eating. Jah popped the champagne, and we continued to eat while sipping our drinks. It was quiet, and this wasn't usually like us. When we were together, we would chat until we couldn't anymore.

"You all right? Mad quiet right now," I broke our silence.

"Yeah, I'm good."

"Okay, if you say so." Taking a bite from the shrimp and broccoli, I continued to eat and get buzzed off this champagne.

"Can I be real with you?"

"Uh, Jah, I thought we've been being real from jump."

"You right."

"What? You got me all worried."

"I want you," he admitted.

My stomach did a huge flop, my breathing got heavier, and my heart was beating out of my chest. The way he stared at me told me that he was serious and wasn't fucking with me. Jah had put his fork down and was now staring into my eyes. If this nigga asked me to marry him, we were going to have some problems.

"Yo-you want me?"

"Yeah, I didn't stutter, did I? Tweeti, since we started fucking around, you got me feeling alive and shit. When I'm not with you, I'm worried about handling business so I can get to you faster. It ain't even about sex, but Lord know I'd tear that pussy up tonight if you let me." He chuckled, which caused me to laugh. "On the real, I feel something for you, and this whole routine we fell into with not talking about our feelings, I wanna stop it. I wanna tell you how I feel and be with you." He reached his hand out and held my hand in his.

"Now, can I be real with you?"

"You already know that, sweetheart."

Smiling, I tried to look away, but he reached up to make sure I stared him right in the eye like he did me.

"I feel the same way about you. It's hard for me to admit my feelings for people because it scares the shit out of me. I've been the girl who has admitted her feelings and got shut down. I . . . I just don't want to get hurt."

He rolled back from the table and rolled over to me. "Tweeti, I'm a lot of things, but real is one thing you never have to question when it comes to me. This shit is hard for me to admit too, but I can't keep acting like you don't mean nothing to me and that I don't wanna be with you. The friend shit is fine, but I wanna be more than friends with you. Shit, I wanna do the nasty in more than one way with you."

Laughing, I hit him in the chest. "You so nasty."

"For real. I wanna be with you, and I don't expect you to tell me today or even tomorrow. Long as you're thinking about it, I'm straight."

"Jah, that girl at the club . . . Who was she?"

"Some shorty that I fucked a few months ago. I ran into her in the club, and we were just kicking it."

"I really feel like you gonna have me out here looking stupid. That's my biggest fear. I'm out here claiming you, and you're making me look stupid as fuck."

"Why the fuck would I do that shit? Shorty was a slut bucket and something to smash. I'm trying to be with you, Tweeti. On my mama, I won't have you out here looking stupid."

When he said it, I believed he wouldn't hurt me or have me out here looking stupid. Jah has been real with me since day one, so why was I so hesitant to give him a chance? Getting hurt wasn't something that you ever wanted, and since I had been hurt before, I wasn't trying to be hurt either.

"Promise?"

"Promise," he told me.

"I guess I'll be your girlfriend or whatever." I rolled my eyes and laughed.

He laughed and pulled me toward him. "Come sit right here." He tapped his lap.

"Uh, do you not see me? I'm not trying to mess up your legs."

"Shut up and come on," he told me. Carefully, I sat on his lap and watched his face. He didn't make any face and held me tightly around the waist. "See, you all scared for what?"

"Your legs buckling," I joked.

"Don't play with me." He pinched me and caused me to laugh. "Give me a kiss," he demanded.

Holding his face, I placed my lips on his and kissed the
hell out of him. It was something that I had been wanting
to do for a long time. "Whew!" I yelled when we broke
our kiss.

"Shit, you got me feeling like I won the lottery or some
shit. Come on, we going to the bedroom." He rolled us
to his bedroom. We weren't going to have sex, but I did
want to cuddle with him and watch our favorite show that
we discovered together. It felt nice to have a man reveal
his feelings for me and be true about them. There was
something special about Jah, and my feelings couldn't
deny that I liked him.

Wynner

My hands were shaking as I held my phone in my hand. If I were stronger, I swear I would be able to snap it in half; *that's* how pissed I was. I'm sure if the nurse came in to check my blood pressure, it would be high as hell. Being in this hospital for two weeks was driving me crazy. The doctors said I had blood clots in my legs and wanted to monitor them before sending me home. Qua had been working so much that I only saw him at night. Even then, he was so tired that he fell asleep in the middle of a conversation between us. Here I was, doing my usual routine, seeing what was going on with *The Shade Room*. There was nothing like having some good messy news to make your day feel a little bit better. Imagine my surprise when my husband was on there with that Instagram model, Olay Vega. Taking a picture is harmless, right? Not when your husband's hand is gripping her ass like Kobe gripping a basketball.

My heart was beating so hard that I was sure I would go into cardiac arrest. Even when I tried to do my breathing exercises, it didn't help. Tears came out of my eyes as I stared at the picture. Qua had this smile on his face that said he was up to no good. When did he go to an event with her to take a picture? All these questions were racing in my head, and I had no one to answer them. Qua had called me earlier and told me that he wouldn't be able to come up here today. Uzi had him going to Miami for a week, so he had to run around and handle things before going. I was so pissed that I was looking in my bed for my phone, and the shit was in my hand the whole time. Dialing his number, I waited for him to answer.

"Babe, you good?"

"No, I'm not. I need you to come now."

"Bet. I'll have Grizz bring me there right away," he told me, and we ended the call.

The good Lord knew how much I loved my husband. More than life I think I loved Qua, but if this nigga was stepping out on me, I was going to lose my mind and go off the handle. I'd given up so much for him, so if he was cheating, then he had to die. When I told him that, he always thought I was joking, but I wasn't. My brothers would do anything to make me happy, and if Qua was out there living foul, then that would be the last time he would be able to live foul. Olay Vega was such a ho and had been with every nigga in the music industry. *Shade Room* was always talking about her and who she was fucking with for the week. How did Qua know her?

It didn't take Qua long to get to the hospital. He rushed in the room like it was an emergency. While waiting for him, I had showered and got dressed. Being in pajamas all day was depressing. When his eyes landed on me, I could see the confusion in them.

"What happened? What are they saying?" He shot each question one after the other. All I could do was smile. The smile was to keep from breaking down and crying. Qua was all I knew, so if he was fucking around on me, I was going to literally lose my mind.

"Nothing happened."

"The fuck, babe? Why you call me like it was an emergency?"

"Imagine my surprise when I go on *Shade Room* and see you gripping another bitch's ass, Quamere!" I tossed my phone at his head. He ducked and picked it up from the floor. The post was still on there. While he looked at the picture, I studied his face. He had this look on his face that told me he really fucked up.

"Oh, this is Olay. I went to support her event she was here to do. We go way back from when we were kids," he tried to explain, like I gave a shit about the bitch.

"Oh yeah? You went to a woman's event to support *without your wife*. I find it really funny how that happened; then you got your hand on her ass."

"Wyn, everything was so fast-paced, so when the photographer pushed her into my arms for a picture, that's how it turned out. On my unborn kids, I didn't put my hand there on purpose."

"Yeah, what the fuck ever. Does she *know* that you're married?"

"Nah, we haven't really got into each other's life like that. Each time we've seen each other, it was in public, and we couldn't really talk. She hit me up and told me she was coming back to New York and would love for me to pop out to her show. So, me and Grizz both went with Sundae."

"You don't see the fucking problem with what you're saying?"

"Nah, what I say?"

"Grizz ain't even with Sundae and thought to bring a chick with him."

"Wynner, you were in the damn hospital!" he barked at me. Usually, he would quiet me, but today, I was in rare form.

"That means you don't go to any damn event, then. You tell that ho that you can't go with her anywhere right now."

"Whatever, Wynner. I know you upset because you're stuck in here, so you about to pick at everything. I told you about Miami, and I'm gonna be away for a week handling business. I love you, and you know I would never do anything to mess up what we have." He came over and kissed me on the forehead.

"I want some," I told him. Sex was the last thing on my mind, but I wanted to see something that had been on my mind. Qua loved me and my body and wouldn't hesitate to fuck me in public. We almost always fucked whenever I was in the hospital.

"Nah, I got to handle some business. We good, right?"

My voice cracked when I spoke. "Yeah."

"What's the matter?"

"Nothing. I'm good." This time, I sounded a bit better. From his expression, he wasn't sold, but Grizz had told him they had to head out.

Kissing me on the forehead again, he headed out, and I broke down crying. I wanted to be released more than anything, and I wanted to be able to be there for my husband. It felt like our marriage was always taking place in a hospital. That statement Qua made when I had to be rushed to the hospital didn't sit well with me. All I wanted was for my husband to want me and not feel like he was going to break me. I had to do something, and I knew exactly what I was going to do. When Qua got down to Miami, I was going to fly down there to surprise him. If they didn't release me, I was going to sign myself out. My marriage was important, and I could feel my husband slipping away from me, despite what he said. I had to fix my marriage before we went down a road neither of us could make it back from.

Uzi

"Nigga, why you sitting like a bitch?" Jah voiced when he rolled into my parents' crib. I came over to speak to my mother about Remi. "Shut the fuck up," I laughed and put my feet down from the couch. "What you doing here?"

"Came to check moms and shit. Where she at?"

"Right here, baby." She came downstairs and hugged Jah. "How are you, Jahquel?"

Jah smirked and rolled to the kitchen. I sent Remi a message and followed them into the kitchen. He was staring in the pots, and my mother knew to go ahead and fix him a plate of whatever the chef had cooked.

"I'm a taken man, Mama," he announced.

"Damn, I was coming to tell her the same thing."

My mother looked from me to Jah and then back at me. "What are you both talking about?"

"Mama, your son found him a good woman," Jah explained. "We been kicking it and shit, and I wanted to make her my girl, so I did."

"When will I get to meet this girl?"

"Chill, Ma. Not yet. Don't wanna scare her away yet. I just got her," Jah joked, but my mother didn't think it was funny.

"And what are you talking about, because last time I saw you, we were talking about Lira." She turned her attention back to me.

"That slut," Jah commented.

"Knock it off," my mama hushed him.

"Her name is Remi, and she's his girlfriend's older sister. Ma, she dope as fuck, man." My mother turned her face, and I knew the drama was about to come.

"Well, let me go see what pops is up to," Jah rolled his ass out of the kitchen when he saw my mother's face.

Soon as he was out of earshot, she started her shit again. "Girlfriend? Parrish, I understand you're grown, but these women don't want you for you."

"She don't want my money, Mama. I really like her."

"Just like you liked, Lira?"

Shaking my head, I knew she was coming with this bullshit. Each time we spoke about something, it always went back to Lira. "Ma, I'm tired of you bringing Lira up into everything. It ain't about her ass right now. I'm telling you that I'm really feeling a woman and you fucking shooting the shit down."

"What makes her so special, Parrish? You never tell me about women that you're dating, so what makes her so special?"

"She shared some shit with me. . . . I see the real her, for real." My mother's face was skeptical as she set down the plate she was preparing for Jah. "Ma, she was raped. She shared that with me, and I felt something inside me. I can't explain it."

"Because she was raped, she's the one?"

"What the fuck? Why would you even say that? I never said she's the one. She might be. Only time will tell if she's the one."

"Parrish, since Lira, a lot has me questioning the women you deal with. It just seems like yest—"

"Stop bringing the shit up every other day!" I barked and stood up. Grabbing my car keys, I headed out the door.

Remi was still at work, and I had to pick her up later. She had been at my crib on and off for the past few weeks. I didn't mind her spending the night because it felt nice having someone lying beside me at night. When I asked Remi to be my girl, it was something that just came out. When it came out, I let it flow to see what she would say. When she said that she would be my girl, a nigga was too happy. Since then, we been chilling and getting to know each other. Remi had a nigga open, and when she wasn't with me, I wanted to know what she was doing. I never felt like this about someone, and Remi had me all the way open.

It was seven at night, and Remi didn't get out of work until nine, so I headed to the club. I knew I shouldn't have been at the club, but I knew I needed to have a drink and see some ass. It was hard to break old habits. When I was usually stressed, I went to the club, had a few drinks, and watched some strippers. My moms had me pissed all the way off, and to avoid saying more shit, I needed to get away from her and clear my mind. I understood she just wanted the best for me, but I'm a grown-ass man and could handle myself. All I wanted her to do was support my decision to be in a relationship. When Jah told her he had a girl, she was all ready to meet Tweeti and shit, but when it's time for me to introduce my chick, she doesn't trust me with picking out women because I used to fuck with Lira. The shit was getting old, and I was going to stop coming the fuck around and telling her my business if she was going to continue with her judgmental shit.

Damn, was this how Wynner felt when I gave her shit about Qua? If this is how she felt, then I needed to calm down on how I acted with Wynner's life. I knew as soon as the thought came across my mind that I was fronting. I wasn't going to stop being me when it came to Wynner. She was the baby, and I wanted to make sure my sis was always taken care of.

When I got to the club, I went straight to the bar. That immature-ass bartender was behind the bar. I ordered my drink and sat around, waiting for the dancers to come out. It was early, but that pussy-nigga Joey wanted to keep the money flowing, so he had these bitches on shift. His best dancers went on later in the night. My phone started buzzing, so I picked it up.

"What's good?"

"Hey, Uzi, I don't need you to pick me up. . . . I'm gonna head home and do something for my mom," she told me.

"You sure?"

"Yeah. I'll come to your house tomorrow. I'm off," she told me.

"A'ight. Text me when you get to the house and take a cab."

"Will do," she replied, and we ended the call.

Since she was doing her own thing tonight, I ordered a bottle to a private section in the front. The bartender promised she would bring it over. The strippers that danced earlier were weak as fuck. Some of them had no damn body on they ass and was stiff as fuck. As I downed my second drink, I looked at the bar and saw her bringing me the bottle.

"Sorry for the wait. . . . I had to take care of a few people. Enjoy." She smiled and left me to do me.

I sat here acting like I was a judge on *American Stripper*. All these bitches were getting the Simon treatment, but they were weak as fuck and weren't doing shit for me. I poured some more into my glass and leaned back while continuing to watch them. My moms was blowing my phone up, but I didn't want to talk. She was the reason my ass ended up here instead of eating the good food that her chef prepared at her crib.

"Uzi, what are you doing here?" Lira interrupted me. Part of me knew she would be here; yet, the other part of

me thought she would leave me alone after the last time
we were together.

"What up?" The liquor was taking over me, and I was
feeling nice as fuck. Even Lira was looking fine as fuck in
the sweat suit she was wearing.

"I'm good. Surprised to see you here." She rolled her
eyes. "Where's your girl?"

"At work, why?"

"So, she *is* your girl?"

"Hell yeah. You asked, and I told your ass, so why you
acting all surprised?"

Lira shook her head and then rolled her eyes. "You
really act like I don't have feelings, Parrish. The way you
treat me like I don't matter fucking hurts."

"How I fucking treat you? Lira, get the fuck out of my
face before I get pissed off."

Batting her eyelashes, she smirked. "Can we go to the
private room? I wanna talk to you."

"Nah."

"I'm gonna go change, do my set, and then I want you
in the back room," she basically told me. Waving over the
bartender, she smirked. "Keep the drinks coming," she
told her.

"On who fucking tab?"

"Mine."

With that, she left to the back, and I sat there chilling. For the next two hours, I watched different strippers come and go. The lights dropped, and Kandle, or
should I say, Lira, came out on the stage. I couldn't
front. Lira was gifted when it came to that pole. While
she danced, it was as if she were dedicating the dance
only to me. My eyes were low as I watched her move
her hips and climb the pole. Shorty had me in a daze
with the art of her climbing that pole and shaking her
ass. My dick was rock hard as I watched her do her

thing. When she was done, she went to the back and then came over my section.

When she grabbed my arm, I knew I should have snatched it back, but I allowed her to pull me up and take me to the back of the club. In the private room, she pushed me onto the couch and unbuckled my pants. My dick was damn near poking through the jeans, wanting her to do whatever she wanted to do. As she was about to put her mouth on my dick, I mushed her head. Remi's face came into my mind, and I couldn't do this shit to her. *I'm* the one who asked her to be with me, and here I was, about to fuck over her trust. The shit would eat me up, and I never really gave a fuck about people's feelings, but I cared about hers.

"What the hell?" Lira screeched. She tried to continue to get to my dick, and I mushed her ass again. I was feeling nice as fuck, so everything seemed like it was happening in slow motion. "What are you doing?"

"Nah, I can't do that to my girl."

"Fuck her. Me and you got history, and I'm 'bout to make you feel good. Remi is a ho anyway," she tried to lie about her.

"*You* the fucking ho. How you calling the bartender the ho? You the one back here trying to suck my dick, knowing I got a girl."

She stood up and put her hands on her hips. "Fuck you, Parrish."

"Kandle, your phone been ringing off the hook," one of the other dancers peeked her head in and told her.

"Nah, you wanna fuck me, but I'll save the beefcake for Remi. Probably one of your niggas calling now." She headed out first, and then I came after her, fixing my jeans. My bottle was nowhere near my section, so I looked at the bar while fixing my pants—and locked eyes with Remi behind the bar. At first, I thought the drinks had me past fucked up, but when I looked back, it was her staring at me with hurt in her eyes.

Rushing over to the bar, I stood there for a minute thinking of my next move. Then, I grabbed her hand as she wiped down the bar. "What the fuck did I tell you?"

"You *really* wanna have this conversation? I just saw you fixing your pants leaving the back room with Kandle. But you asked *me* to be your girl. Why? So you could continue to fuck that slut?" She snatched her hand away and went back to work.

"Didn't I tell you I didn't want you back here?"

"Leave me alone. You're not paying my bills, so when Joey asked me to step in, I told him yeah. Bye."

She didn't expect me to hop the damn bar and drag her ass from behind the fucking bar. I was drunk as fuck; still, I knew what the fuck I was doing. Remi didn't make a scene or kick and scream as I dragged her out of the club. As we headed out, I noticed Joey's corny ass standing there with his mouth shut. His ass wasn't going to say shit unless he wanted to get his face knocked the fuck off. My car was parked out front like always. Handing Remi my keys, I turned to her.

"Drive us to my crib," I demanded.

"I'll drive you home, but I'll be back."

I jumped at her, and she dared me to do it again. "Rem, don't play with me."

"We're not going to work out. It's obvious you still wanna fuck Kandle, so I'ma let you do you."

She pressed the button to start the car, then fixed the chair. As she was about to pull off, Kandle came frantically banging on my window. "See, this is too fucking much. Y'all belong together!" Remi yelled as she hit the steering wheel. "I *dare* you to open that damn window," she challenged me like I was about to listen.

Pressing the button, I rolled down the window.

"Parris—"

"Bitch, his name is fucking Uzi. Stop calling him Parrish like you his bitch. I'm tired of your shit. You been wanting to throw your weight around like this nigga is yours. He's *my* nigga, and it's clear because *I'm* the one behind the wheel of his whip!" Remi barked and hit me at the same time.

"Bitch, mind your fucking business. . . . You're behind the wheel of his car, that's fine, but *I* have his daughter. My mama just called, and Paris got into an accident," Lira revealed.

"A *daughter?*" Remi screamed.

Everything was spinning as I held on to Remi's arm and the car handle. "My dayfjsvns," I slurred as everything went black.

To Be Continued . . .